FLIGHT OF BETRAYAL

ALSO BY MIKE PAULL

Tales from the Sky Kitchen Cafe

FLIGHT OF BETRAYAL

Mike Paull

Published by Skyhawk Publishing

Printed in the USA

Design by Carla Resnick

ISBN 9780985874308

Library of Congress Catalog Number 2012912335

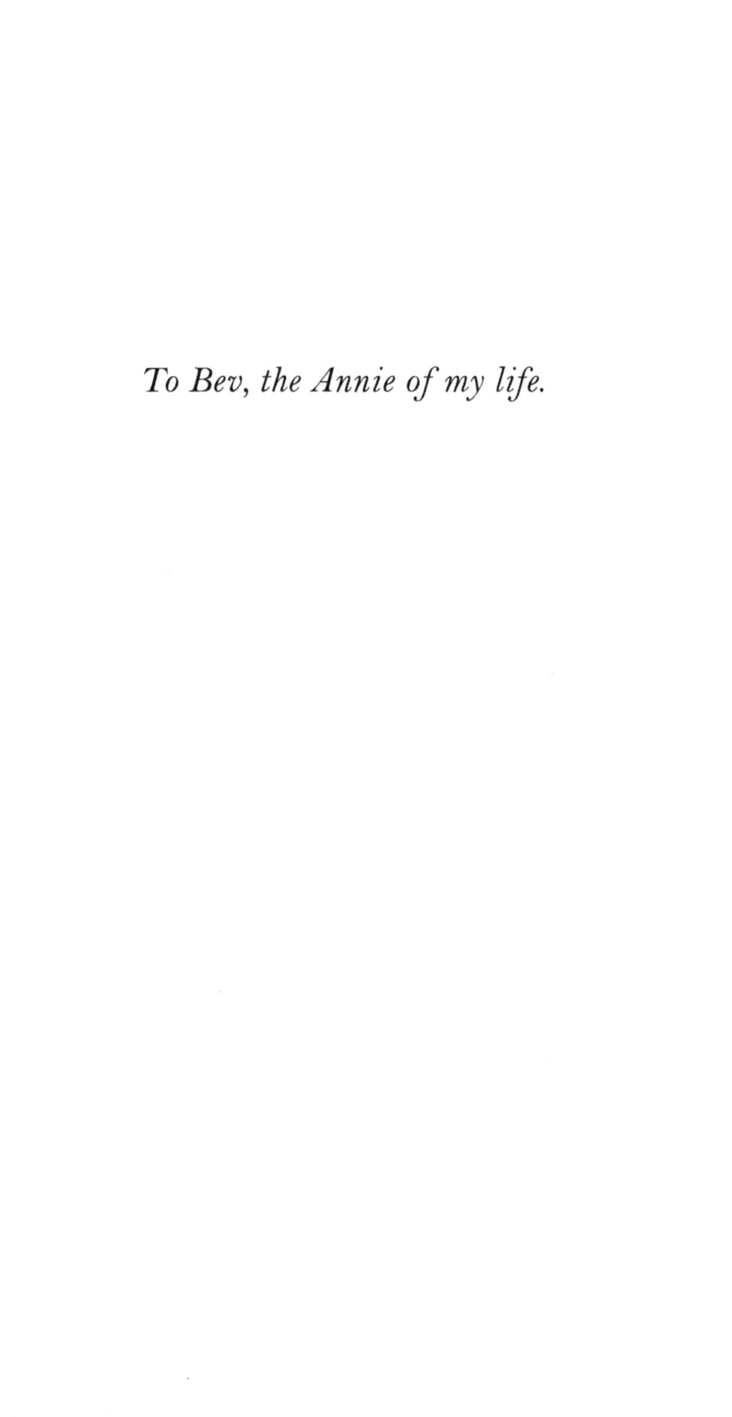

To Bev, the Annie of my life.

*"When you have eliminated all which
is impossible, then whatever remains,
however improbable, must be the truth."*

—Arthur Conan Doyle,
"The Case-Book of Sherlock Holmes"

FLIGHT OF BETRAYAL

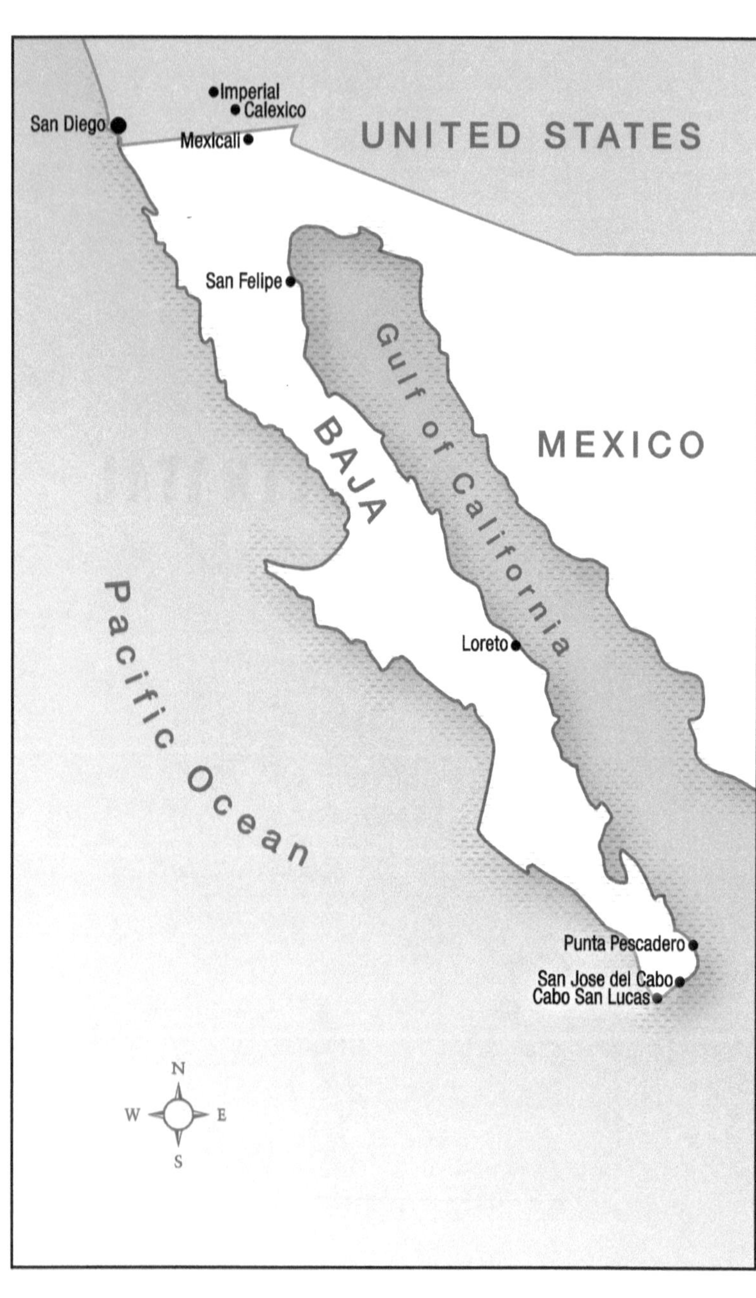

Imperial
Calexico
San Diego
Mexicali
UNITED STATES
San Felipe
Gulf of California
BAJA
MEXICO
Pacific Ocean
Loreto
Punta Pescadero
San Jose del Cabo
Cabo San Lucas
N
W
E
S

Prologue

Brett began braking for the stop sign ahead. The only lights on the street were from a front porch, his headlights, and those of a pickup truck a hundred yards behind. As he stopped at the sign he glanced into his rear view mirror, and to his horror, he saw the lights of the truck accelerating toward him. Before he could get his Porsche into low gear, the pickup rammed into his rear end and his head was snapped back from the impact of the large truck with his small sports car.

Two men jumped out of the cab, yanked Brett out of his car and threw him to the ground. He could make out the size of his attackers. One was very tall and lean; the other was short with muscles bulging from his short sleeve t-shirt.

The short one kicked Brett in the right ribcage. Brett heard a crack and rolled into a fetal position. The tall guy yelled, "Get up, Raven." Brett groaned and rolled onto his stomach, but the pain radiating from his midsection wouldn't allow him to push himself up. The short guy grabbed the back of his shirt and yanked him to his feet.

While the muscular attacker propped him against the side of the car, the tall one grabbed his left arm and growled, "Some friends of yours wanted to send you this little message. Keep your nose out of other people's business." He took hold of Brett's thumb and slowly pushed it toward his wristwatch as Brett screamed out in pain. The man just kept pushing until Brett could feel the tendons and ligaments tear as his thumb bent back to meet his wrist. He passed out.

When he awoke he was in a hospital bed and groggy from drugs, but he did his best to take stock of his condition. He had a cast on his left thumb and wrist, his midsection was taped from his nipples to just above his belly button, he could feel a large bump on his forehead and his neck was so sore he couldn't move his head. He had an IV inserted into to the top of his right hand, which was receiving fluid from a vinyl sack hanging from a metal stand. Another tube was attached to an oxygen source in the wall and led to a cannula strapped under his nose.

The drugs kicked in again and Brett began to

doze off. As he drifted back into sleep he struggled to recount the events that had brought him to this time and place.

PART ONE

THE CRASH

Chapter One

The receptionist picked up the phone on the first ring. "Dr. Raven's office, this is Ginger."

"Ginger, it's Annie, I have to talk to Brett right away. It can't wait."

Ginger responded to the urgency in her voice. "Hold on, Annie, I'll get him."

Brett was in the treatment room finishing up on his last dental patient of the day, when he spotted Ginger signaling him. He slipped off his gloves and took the note from her hand. He read it, pulled down his mask and turned to his assistant. "Janet, would you help Mrs. Granger rinse? I have to take a call."

He closed the door to his private office, pushed the lighted button on the phone panel and picked up the receiver. "Annie, what's wrong?"

Annie's voice was shaking. "Brett, J.T. is dead! He crashed the plane on the way home from a fishing trip in Baja."

Brett could taste the bile in his throat rising from the knot in his stomach. "Oh God, I'll be right over."

J.T. had been Brett's friend, until he married Annie, Brett's ex-wife. They were still able to remain partners in the twin engine Beechcraft Baron, which they flew out of San Carlos, an airport located thirty miles south of San Francisco. J.T. had been a pilot ten years longer than Brett, and he had been the one who had encouraged him to take up flying. He knew everything there was to know about flying and everything there was to know about their airplane. Brett was incredulous that J.T. could crash the Baron.

It took Brett only ten minutes to reach Annie's house. She opened the door and collapsed into his arms. Brett held her tight. When he relaxed his grip he asked, "How did you find out? Who called?"

"A guy from the FAA called about an hour ago." Tears streamed down her face. "He said the plane went down thirty miles south of San Felipe. There was a horrendous fire and both J.T. and his passenger were burned beyond recognition."

Brett helped Annie to the couch and went over to the bar. He poured two generous glasses of Chevas and handed one to Annie, who by now was quivering every time she inhaled. The Scotch settled her down and within ten minutes she was able to raise her shoulders and speak a few words. "How is it possible? He's flown to Mexico dozens of times. He could fly that trip with his eyes closed."

"How was his health, had he been to the doctor recently? Maybe he had a heart attack."

"He never said anything. I know he was under a lot of stress with his business, but he was only fifty-two and you know in what great shape he kept himself."

Brett's brain was working overtime trying to make sense out of this tragedy. He knew pilot error was the number one cause of airplane accidents; mechanical failure, the fear which most passengers harbor, was a distant second. It would be months before the NTSB (National Transportation Safety Board) would finish its investigation and write its report. Brett also knew that often, when no obvious cause was found, the board would assume pilot error and close the case.

Fatigue had set in for Annie; however, Brett sensed that sleep would not come easily. He went to the medicine cabinet, found a bottle of Ambien and took out a five milligram tablet. He gave it to Annie along with a splash of the Scotch and convinced her to lie down on her bed. He turned off the light as he quietly closed the door and returned to the living room, where he poured himself another Scotch and sat down to think.

Chapter Two

In 1976 Brett was a freshman at UC Berkeley. During a Friday night fraternity party, he and his roommate Rob were perched on the staircase eyeing the door and checking out the female talent.

Rob spotted a prospect. "How about that one with the tight blue sweater?"

"Not my type, too sexy looking." Brett replied.

"Man, you're picky. How about the tall one with all the jewelry?"

"Too hard looking."

Rob was running out of patience. "There's a prospect, the cute one with the short hair and the neat figure."

Brett turned his head toward the direction in which Rob was looking. Once he spotted her he couldn't take his eyes off her. He could tell she was only about five feet tall and didn't weigh more than a hundred pounds. She glanced in his direction and Brett gave her a big smile. Her green eyes lit up and she smiled back. "See ya later, Rob." Brett said, as he headed in her direction.

Brett moved toward the door and intercepted her as she picked up her name tag. "Hi, I'm Neil Diamond, welcome to my concert."

Annie's smile turned into full fledged laughter as she thrust out her hand. "Nice to meet you Neil, I'm Annie Frazier."

After an hour on the dance floor and a lot of small talk, Brett led Annie toward the soft drinks. "Let's grab a couple cokes and go up to my room. I can spike 'em up with some rum."

Annie looked disappointed. "I don't think so. I thought maybe you were interested in me, but it looks like you just want to get laid."

Brett's face flushed. "I am interested in you. I... I'm really sorry. I didn't mean to come on like that."

"Well you did. There're plenty of girls here with horns, if that's what you're looking for."

"Annie please, what can I do to make up for that remark?"

"Nothing," she said as she walked away.

Brett felt ashamed and didn't follow her to the door. Instead he slowly climbed the stairs to his room and went to bed.

A month later, he was in the library with his head buried in a book, when he felt a tap on his shoulder.

"Well if it isn't Neil Diamond."

Brett looked up. "Annie, it's great to see you. I'm so sorry about..."

She interrupted him. "Come on Brett that was a month ago. How about you buy me a burger and maybe I'll let you apologize a couple more times."

He dropped two books off the table while scrambling to gather his things. "Let's go."

Annie wrapped her arm around his and they headed to Larry Blake's Steakhouse.

They sat at the corner table for three and a half hours. This time there was no small talk. They talked about their goals and their visions for the future. "How long does it take to become a dentist?" Annie asked.

"Depends, hopefully only four years here, and then another four in dental school."

"How about you? Will you have a teaching credential in four years?"

"I plan to, I'll have to student teach during my fourth year."

The waiter started circling the table, asking if they needed anything else, before Annie realized how late it was. "I think he wants to go home."

Brett laughed and picked up the check.

Annie reached in her purse. "I was only kidding about the free burger. I want to split the bill."

They had a tug of war with the check until Brett finally wrestled it free and dropped a ten dollar bill on the table.

Brett walked Annie back to the dorm. They

stood awkwardly at the front door until Brett finally leaned over and gave her a kiss on the cheek. "Thanks, Annie. I'm sorry for being such an asshole at the party."

She put her arms around his neck, pulled him toward her, and gave him a kiss on the lips. "I figured you were worth a second chance." She said as she disappeared through the door.

They dated each other exclusively for the entire freshman year. During the sophomore year Brett broached the subject. "I think you should go to the student health center and get birth control pills."

Annie turned crimson. "I'm embarrassed."

"Come on Annie its 1977, all the girls are taking them. I'll go with you."

Once their relationship became more serious, they began talking about marriage and family. "How many kids do you want?" Brett asked.

"We both grew up without siblings and we know how lonely that can be. I want our kids to enjoy sisters or brothers."

"So what does that mean, six or seven?'

Annie laughed. "No, but at least two, maybe three. How about you?"

"As long as you don't mind pumping them out we can have as many as you want."

Before the senior year began Brett and Annie had rented an apartment together. It was like playing house until lightening struck. The pill had been giving Annie cramps and the doctor took her off it for three months, making it Brett's responsibility to provide protection. One night he reached into the drawer only to find there were no packets left in the box. He talked her into it. "It's only one time, it'll be okay."

Two months later Annie announced she had missed a period. They went to the doctor together. She was pregnant.

The mood in the apartment immediately changed. It wasn't playing house anymore, it wasn't hypothetical talk about how big a family to have; it was a real life decision.

Annie was distraught. "We never should have taken the chance. I'm ashamed of myself for being so stupid."

"Don't blame yourself. I'm the one who talked you into it." After a long silence Brett spoke again. "I don't see how you can keep it."

"Why not?"

"Our plans, our dreams, they would go up in flames. You wouldn't be able to teach and I would have to forget about dental school. What kind of marriage will we have if we start it out that way?"

"But I have a baby growing inside of me. I want to give birth to it."

"It's not like you'll never get pregnant again. We can still have those kids we talked about."

Annie wanted him to tell her she should have the baby and they would find a way to handle it, but he didn't. She had begun to cry and blew her nose on a Kleenex. "I don't know if I can go through with an abortion."

Brett put his arm around her shoulder. "I'll help you through it."

She pushed his arm away. "I need time to think about it." She said, as she got up, ran to the bedroom and buried her head in the pillow. A week passed and Annie was still clinging to the hope that Brett would come to her with a way to keep the baby, but he never did.

The subject went underground for another two days until one evening Brett asked, "What have you decided?"

Annie didn't hesitate, "I want to keep it."

Brett became analytical. "Annie, put your emotions aside for a minute and look at this long term. If you give up the baby, our life will come back to where it was and in a few years we can have children at a time when we can handle them."

Brett's cold approach angered Annie. "The baby is just an inconvenience to you, isn't it? You're worried you might have to work a little harder to get to where you want to be."

Now Brett got angry with her. "That's not fair. It's not just where I want to be, it's where we want to be."

The argument kept going into the early hours of the morning. As it dragged on, Annie began to feel as if she were a fly trapped between the strands of a spider's web; the more desperately she tried to break free, the deeper she became entwined. Finally her energy was depleted and she surrendered to its grip. "Let's get it over with tomorrow."

Annie was silent on the ride home from the clinic. She felt physically empty, emotionally drained, and resentful toward Brett for putting his career ahead of her feelings. For more than two weeks Annie remained withdrawn and overwhelmed with feelings of sadness. She wanted to share her feelings with Brett, but kept them to herself, because she sensed he didn't want to hear or try to understand them.

The next three months remained very quiet in the little apartment. Luckily midterms were approaching, and their attention became focused on getting through them with good grades. Neither Brett nor Annie was really sure their relationship was going to survive until a letter arrived, which like an electric charge to the heart, jolted their life back into rhythm.

The return address was from the University of California Medical Center and it arrived by certified mail. Annie opened it and ran down the hall to the bedroom. "You got in, you got in. You start in the fall."

Brett looked at the letter in disbelief. "We're

going to be okay; everything we talked about is going to happen." He gave Annie a hug. "It's time to think about getting married."

The wedding was only two weeks before the start of the fall semester, and the closest they came to a honeymoon was looking through travel magazines and agreeing that someday they'd go to Italy.

Brett worked hard in school; however, it was Annie who took on the burden of supporting the family. She camped out at the school district office everyday until they finally gave her an interview and proceeded to hire her on the spot. She brought home the monthly paycheck and set up their budget which enabled them to regularly save enough for the following semester's tuition.

Brett graduated in the spring of 1984 and in September, at the age of twenty-six, he opened his dental practice in San Carlos, a bedroom community on the San Francisco Peninsula. They decided Annie wouldn't go back to teaching; instead, she would use her organizational skills to take on the duties as receptionist and manager of Brett's office.

Two patients called for appointments the first week. Annie asked Brett when to schedule them. "Put them both in Wednesday at nine o'clock." Brett responded.

"Are you kidding, the whole week is open for

appointments. Why would you schedule your only two patients at the same time?"

Brett gave out a sly laugh. "With both of them in the reception room at the same time, they'll think I'm really busy. Give it a try."

On Wednesday morning Annie looked at Brett as he prepared for his first patients. His olive skin and dark hair were a striking contrast against the blue scrubs and white clinic jacket he wore.

Brett caught Annie admiring him and put his arms around her. "You've given up a lot to get me here. I owe you for all your sacrifices and I'm going to make it up to you."

Annie smiled. "I hope so, I really do."

Chapter Three

After the funeral about thirty people came back to Annie's house. Her mother had arranged for a caterer and Brett had set up a bar. The topic of conversation was predictable; how could this have happened to J.T.? Annie held up well and by four o'clock everyone had given their condolences and had slipped away. Annie's mother was rinsing dishes in the kitchen and looked up when Brett brought in some dirty wine glasses. "What?" Brett asked.

"What ever happened between you and Annie? I had never seen two people more in love." Brett couldn't answer and wiped the corner of his eye as he went back to the living room for the rest of the glasses.

When Annie's mother left at six-thirty, Brett and Annie sat down on the couch, each with a glass of wine. After five minutes of silence, Annie turned to Brett. "Brett, I'm embarrassed to admit it, but I have no idea about our finances. I know J.T. was having financial problems and I don't know if he left more debts than money. Could you look through his records and help me sort them out?"

Brett looked surprised. "J.T. was a financial advisor. He must have discussed personal finances with you."

Annie's face became tight. "Something was wrong the last year or two, he was very distant. We didn't talk much and he started to sleep in the extra bedroom. You know I never loved J.T. the way I loved you. God how I wish I could turn the clock back five years."

Brett wasn't ready for this conversation.

"Why don't you soak in a hot bath? I'll go into J.T.'s office and see if I can start figuring things out for you."

Brett sat down at J.T.'s desk, slipped off his tie and unbuttoned the top of his dress shirt. He noticed in addition to the desk, there were two main file cabinets. The large one contained the records for about two hundred and fifty business clients, and the smaller one contained personal records that, Brett assumed, would help with Annie's concerns.

He opened the top drawer of the desk. Two check books were lying side by side. One was a large leather case with three checks on each page. It was obviously the business register. The other was a small vinyl case and had the usual single checks most people use for personal finances.

As Brett opened the small check book, a shiver went up his spine. He felt like a voyeur, looking at scenes he had no right see. J.T. had once been his best friend, but he had never shared his personal financial information.

He flipped through the check register. All of the checks had been written for the usual household expenses one would expect. The last check written two days before J.T. departed for Mexico left a balance of $75.97 in the check book; it was not a balance he had expected to find in the account of a financial advisor.

Brett opened the business check book. The register was very long and he knew it would take several hours to examine it thoroughly; however, the last entry caught his attention. The day before J.T. had left for Mexico he had written a check for $10,000 made out to cash. Why did he do that, and where is the cash? He certainly didn't place it in his household account and he would have known better than to take that much cash to Mexico. Brett ran his hand through his hair as he pondered where J.T. would have put that money.

He heard Annie moving about in the living room and thought this would be a good time to hang it up for the evening. Before he got up from the desk, he felt he should take a look in the file cabinet that contained J.T.'s personal files. He pulled open the first drawer and right on top was a folder labeled LIFE INSURANCE. Brett opened the folder and looked inside.

Annie was sitting on the couch sipping a glass of Chardonnay. Brett poured himself a glass of wine, dropped the folder on the coffee table, and sat down beside her. "Annie, I don't think you have anything to worry about. J.T. left you a life insurance policy worth $5 million."

Chapter Four

Chapter Four

Brett met J.T. in the spring of 1989, five years after he had gone into practice. A brochure arrived in the mail from Talbot Financial, a consulting firm specializing in financial planning and investments. A free seminar was planned at the Hyatt Regency in Burlingame, a few miles north of Brett's office. He reserved a spot for both himself and Annie.

The speaker at the seminar was John Thomas Talbot, the owner of the firm. Brett and Annie immediately took a liking to him. He was a handsome guy about ten years older than Brett with a charismatic personality. Standing about six foot three, Talbot was a good five inches taller than Brett and in contrast to Brett's dark features, he had blue eyes and wavy blond hair.

Although Talbot displayed an impressive physical presence, it was his demeanor which captured his audience. He was organized, confident, and believable. His philosophy of financial planning and investing was different from any of the other speakers Brett and Annie had previously heard. Talbot didn't try to sell the audience stocks or bonds or life insurance, instead he talked about goals; where do you want to be ten years, twenty years and thirty years from now and how can he help get you there? He talked about levels of risk and the importance of an investor to be able to sleep at night without worry. After listening to him for forty-five minutes, Brett thought that John Thomas Talbot might be the smartest guy he had ever heard.

John Talbot's background was far different from both Brett's and Annie's. They had come from middle class families. Brett's dad had died, when he was sixteen; however, along with some insurance money and a good secretarial job, his mother was able to provide for them. Annie's dad was a journeyman lawyer, who had never gotten rich, but was able to keep his family very comfortable.

Talbot had it tough. His family was poor. His dad was an unlicensed electrician, who when John was three years old, had grabbed the wrong wire and had never worked again. The family lived on a small disability check and some housecleaning money his mother was able to make from time to time.

Luckily John Thomas Talbot had two things going for him. He was smart and he was an athlete. He went to school in South San Francisco, earned a straight 4.0 average and broke every conference record for a high school quarterback. Stanford, just down the road in Palo Alto, offered him a scholarship and he jumped at it.

On his first day at Stanford he wrote down three objectives: first—always plan ahead, second—always weigh the consequences, good or bad, for decisions, and third and most important—work hard for success and never become poor again.

Brett and Annie waited until all the others had left the seminar room before they approached Talbot. Brett thrust out his hand. "Mr. Talbot, I'm Brett Raven and this is my wife, Annie. We'd like to buy you dinner tonight."

"Let's get going, I'm hungry. By the way, call me J.T." he replied.

Brett and Annie owned a beautiful townhouse on the top of the ridge overlooking the city of San Carlos. The main floor housed both the living and dining rooms as well as the kitchen. An extra bedroom completed that level. The entire second floor was devoted to a master bedroom suite and an extra room, which Brett and Annie used as an office. The views were spectacular. All of the windows faced east and south, providing them with a panorama of the entire bay from San Francisco to San Jose. Since they hadn't yet started a family, it was perfect for their lifestyle.

After their dinner with J.T. they had set a date for him to come by the house to describe his financial services. Friday was the day during the week Annie and Brett had off together, and usually they would make plans to spend it in San Francisco or take a three day road trip up or down the coast; however, this Friday they stayed at home for their appointment with J.T. Talbot.

At exactly one o'clock, J.T. swung his BMW 735iL into their driveway. Annie flashed her gorgeous smile as she greeted him at the door. "Hi, J.T., are you always this prompt?"

Just as expected, J.T. was perfectly dressed in a navy blue blazer, a powder blue dress shirt open at the neck, grey slacks, and tan tassel loafers. "I try to be. I don't want to keep people waiting like those damned dentists do."

Annie laughed and said. "Come on in. Brett's in the living room, I'll get the coffee."

Annie poured coffee as J.T. opened his briefcase and spread several papers over the table. He reviewed his philosophy and his services as well as his fees, and then he took out a ten page pamphlet. "I want you guys to fill in all the data requested. It's going to be a pain in the ass, but try to be accurate, because I'm going to create a financial plan from it."

Brett and Annie promised to have the data pamphlet in the mail to him in a week. J.T. suggested their next meeting be at his home where he had his business office; they scheduled it the Friday after next. Annie and Brett walked J.T. to the door and watched him fire up the BMW. As they closed the door they looked at each other and almost in unison said, "Damn he's smart."

J.T.'s house was located in Atherton, a wealthy community five miles south of San Carlos. All the lots were a minimum one acre in size; some were as big as five acres. The front yard was all grass surrounded by a circular driveway. The house itself was an English Tudor and was nestled under giant oak trees. A peak into the back yard revealed a swimming pool with a brick patio.

The inside of the house was equally spectacular. The square footage appeared to be close to five thousand. To go with the Tudor style there were heavy dark wood beams exposed throughout the rooms. The kitchen and baths had all been remodeled and displayed beautiful granite counters.

Annie took it all in and asked, "Do you live here all by yourself?"

J.T. laughed. "That's the first question everyone asks. I've had female companionship from time to time, but it never seems to work out."

J.T.'s private office was a perfect fit for the house. The room was about twenty by twenty, had dark wood cabinets, and a floor to ceiling bookcase with a brass sliding ladder that covered an entire wall. A large antique desk and three soft leather swivel chairs, one for J.T, and two for his clients, were situated in the middle of the room. In contrast to the dark wood, the room was finished off with a white Berber carpet.

J.T. gave both Annie and Brett a plastic covered folder containing all the information he was going to cover. He started by reviewing their financial goals for the next ten, twenty and thirty years. He began his presentation on how he would help them reach those goals.

"The first step we have to take is to get you into the proper business structure. Because a corporate structure offers more tax benefits and because it allows a deduction for a retirement plan, I want Brett to become a professional corporation. Once we have that established, we will set up what's called a Pension and Profit Sharing Trust. It will allow you to set aside up to $30,000 a year and deduct it from your income. All the money you invest within the trust will grow free of taxes."

Annie raised her hand the way a first grader would. "How are we going to get away without paying taxes?"

J.T. smiled, "You don't get away without paying taxes. When you retire and start drawing the money out, then you'll pay the taxes. The advantage of this structure allows you to invest every dollar and get earnings which you can reinvest and not pay taxes on until you retire. It's called the tax free compounding of money."

Brett joined in. "It sounds too easy."

"Well it's not that easy. You still have to earn enough to put away that much money," J.T. continued. "Anyway, once we have that in place, I want you to increase your Office Overhead and Disability Insurance. With the amount of insurance you have right now, if you were unable to work, your income would be decreased by 80%. Annie wouldn't be able to afford that silk blouse she's wearing. As a matter of fact you wouldn't be able to pay the mortgage."

Both Brett and Annie were thinking the same thing. Thank God we found this guy.

J.T. didn't miss a beat. "The next area we have to address is your personal structure. We're going to get you together with a lawyer and set up wills and living trusts. I know you guys are young, but we're all going to die. When that happens you want the best protection for the one who's left behind."

J.T. could see it was getting a little overwhelming. "Hey, how about a coke or a beer?"

Annie and Brett both raised a finger.

"Which?" J.T. asked.

"Beer," they said in unison.

J.T. opened a cabinet which contained a small bar refrigerator. He popped the caps off two Pale Ales and opened a coke for himself.

Brett took a pull from the bottle. "Is that it?

"One more thing. Everybody hates to buy it, but Brett needs life insurance."

"J.T., I'm only thirty-one years old."

He had heard that response dozens of times before. "That's exactly the point. At thirty-one, the policy is cheap and you can afford it. Brett's income accounts for 95% of your combined total, Annie's only accounts for 5%. If something happens to you, Annie will be left with nothing. I'm sure you two will be starting a family soon. You have to have protection." J.T. leaned back, put both hands behind his neck and said, "Now we're done."

J.T. walked them to their car. "How would you two like to go to Lake Tahoe for lunch tomorrow?"

Annie had a quizzical look. "Drive eight hours for a sandwich?"

J.T. knew she would take the bait. "I don't think that will be necessary. I have a plane at the San Carlos Airport. It only takes about forty five minutes to get there."

Brett turned to Annie. "You up for it?"

"You bet." Annie replied.

The next day J.T. drove Brett and Annie to a large hangar on the west side of the airport. He slid the doors open to reveal a sleek red, white, and blue twin engine airplane. It was a Beechcraft Baron B55, nicknamed the "Baby Baron" because it only had five seats and two small 260 horsepower engines. For the smallest in the fleet, it was very quick. J.T. consistently got 180 knots, about 207 miles per hour, out of it.

J.T. attached a motor tow to the nose wheel and eased the baron out of the hangar. He closed the doors and began a pre-flight inspection. He walked around the plane checking the fuel, oil, wings, tail and underside. When he was satisfied that everything looked good, he waved and said, "Let's jump in."

Annie got in first through the single door on the right side of the plane, and settled into one of the back seats. J.T. entered next and took the left pilot seat. Brett was the last one to get in and he took the right co-pilot seat. J.T. reached in front of Brett and said, "Let me lock the door, I don't want to take off with that open."

J.T. put on a set of headphones and Brett and Annie did the same. He took out a long check list and handed it to Brett. "You read each item and I'll respond to it."

It took about five minutes to check all the items on the list. The second to last item Brett read was, "left engine."

J.T. responded. "Start." The left engine roared to life.

Brett read the last item. "Right engine."

"Start," and the second engine began to hum in unison with the other.

J.T. received clearance to taxi and guided the plane to a run up area next to the runway.

After checking both engines and their gauges in the run-up area, J.T. switched to the tower frequency. "Baron seven, seven, seven, three, Romeo is ready to go on runway three zero, right downwind departure."

"Baron, triple seven, three, Romeo cleared for takeoff.

"Cleared for takeoff, seven, three Romeo."

J.T. taxied the Baron onto the runway, lined up with the centerline, put his feet on the brakes, and advanced the throttles to full power. The airplane felt like a chained animal who wanted to run. J.T. released the brakes, and as the Baron screamed down the runway Brett felt a rush of exhilaration.

Just as promised, J.T. greased the Baron onto runway two eight in Truckee, forty-seven minutes from the time they left San Carlos.

Annie and Brett watched J.T. attach tie down chains to the airplane, after which they all started walking toward the terminal. "How do we get to the lake? It's over the ridge." Brett asked J.T.

"Follow me." J.T. said as he led them to the parking lot.

J.T. stopped in front of a fifteen year old Jeep Wagoneer. It wasn't very attractive. It had a boxy shape and its four doors and tailgate were covered with wood simulated decals. J.T. reached under the left wheel well and pulled out a set of keys. "Get in," he said.

Twenty minutes later they were in Tahoe City, sitting on the deck of Jakes On The Lake, overlooking the marina on the northern edge of Lake Tahoe with the Sierra Nevada Mountains in the background. The water that day was deep blue and with no wind blowing was as smooth as glass.

The trio spent about two hours over lunch. Brett and Annie had a couple beers, but J.T. only drank coke. He was following the FAA rules which required: eight hours between bottle and throttle. By four o'clock they were back in San Carlos putting the plane away in the hangar. As they walked back to the car, Brett turned to J.T. "I'd like to learn how to fly; how do I start?"

J.T. could have predicted it. "See that little

diner across the field? Meet me there for lunch tomorrow."

Brett made a point of finishing up his patient before noon. He walked into the Sky Kitchen Cafe, spotted J.T. at a counter in the center of the restaurant and took the seat that was saved for him. It wasn't easy getting a seat at the center counter. Although the Sky Kitchen had room for about fifty customers, the center counter only seated twelve, and it was there that the local pilots congregated. Every lunch hour they jockeyed for a coveted spot.

The camaraderie at the counter was electric. All the pilots knew each other and talked flying for the entire hour and a half. The passion for flying he experienced that day made Brett want to be a part of this fraternity.

J.T. turned to the guy sitting on his other side. "Brett, this is Jim, he's going to be your flight instructor."

Brett took to flying with a vengeance. He flew four times a week with Jim and usually twice a week with J.T. In four months he had earned his private pilot certificate.

Brett, Annie and J.T. started to take flying trips together. Almost every Friday they would load up the Baron and take off for the weekend. Once in awhile J.T. would bring along a blonde with long legs, a large chest, and a small intellect; however, he seemed to enjoy himself more when just the three of them made the trips. They were together so often the pilots at the Sky Kitchen nicknamed them the Three Musketeers.

A year after he received his private license, Brett passed the check ride for an instrument rating.

J.T. called Brett at the office. "Hi Ginger, this is J.T. Talbot."

"Oh, hello Mr. Talbot, Dr. Raven is with a patient right now. Would you like me to have him call you?"

"No, just ask him to meet me at the British Bankers Club in Menlo Park at about five-thirty. I have a proposition he can't resist."

"I'll tell him." Ginger replied.

J.T., who never drank when he was working or flying, was sitting at the English style bar sipping a dry Bombay martini when Brett flopped on the stool next to him. J.T. caught the bartender's eye and lifted a single finger. By the time Brett removed his jacket, a martini was on the bar in front of him.

"What's the occasion? Brett asked. "Ginger made it sound like I was going to inherit some money."

J.T. smiled. "Just the opposite, I want to relieve you of some. I looked at a Baron 58 today, it's gorgeous. The two engines are bigger than the ones on my 55 and the interior is much larger. In addition to the door for the pilot and co-pilot, there are two double side doors. They enter into the passenger area where two pairs of seats face each other with a small fold down table in between. It trues out at 200 knots, which means we'd be traveling at 230 miles per hour."

"What do you mean, we?" Brett asked, as he winced from the gulp of alcohol going down his throat.

"I want you to be my partner in it."

Brett choked on the martini. "J.T., I only have three hundred hours and no multi-engine license."

"Big deal, you fly as well as guys with a thousand hours. Jim will get you trained for the multi-engine check ride. You can use my 55 to train in. The new plane won't be available for three months anyway."

Brett's pulse started to quicken. The thought of piloting a machine like the 58 was overwhelming. "What's it going to cost?"

"It's a 1975 model, so its sixteen years old, but it has two new engines and all new avionics. We can get it for $150,000, $75,000 each."

Brett knew he wanted to do it, but he replied. "That's a lot of money; I better talk it over with Annie."

"No problem. I didn't expect you to say yes without talking to her." J.T. hesitated for a moment and then said, "Brett I envy what you and Annie have together. I only hope some day I'll find a woman like her. You're a lucky guy."

When Brett walked into the townhouse, Annie was prepping veggies for a stir fry. "So what was

J.T. so eager to talk to you about?"

"Oh, nothing important."

Annie broke into laughter. "You never were a good bull shitter. Come on, what did he want?"

"He wants us to buy one half of a 58 Baron."

Annie's mouth fell open. "Oh my God, isn't that the big one with the double side doors and the club seating?"

"That's it."

"Are we going to do it?"

"Do you want to?"

Annie threw her arms around Brett's neck. "I know you do and that's good enough for me."

Brett gave her a big kiss.

On the afternoon of June 19th, 1991 Brett and J.T. pushed the Baron 58 into the hangar for the first time. That was the beginning of four wonderful years for the Three Musketeers.

They traveled everywhere together. Their trips took them as far east as the Bahamas, and as far north as Alaska. Their favorite trip, however, was going south to Baja Mexico, and their favorite destination was Punta Pescadero—a small resort about sixty miles north of Cabo San Lucas. It was located on the gulf side of Baja, commonly know as the Sea of Cortez, and it had one of the few paved and secure private runways on the peninsula. Each of the twenty rooms had a view of the sea and a sunken fireplace. The dining room, pool and bar all overlooked the sea, where snorkeling and deep sea fishing were always available to the guests. Once in awhile J.T. would bring one of his tall blondes, along on the trip; however, as usual, he always seemed to have a better time when it was just the three of them.

Chapter Five

It had been a week since the funeral and Brett had made a point of going by Annie's house everyday to make sure she was holding up alright. He got out of the office at five-thirty and gave her a call. "How would you like Chinese tonight?"

"I don't think so; I really haven't had much of an appetite."

"How about I pick some up anyway? I'll be over to your house in about an hour."

Annie sounded pretty down. "Whatever you want."

Brett drove up the circular driveway leading to the English Tudor. He parked his Porsche in front of the house, grabbed the brown paper bag packed with food and rang the bell.

Annie opened the door and gestured for him to come in. She didn't look good. She wore an old pair of warm up pants with a sloppy sweatshirt.

Her hair wasn't brushed back and it looked as if it hadn't been washed in a couple days. Her eyes were red and swollen from crying.

"Can we talk about it?" Brett asked.

They sat down in the living room and Annie replied, "Brett, I know my marriage to J.T. was a mistake. He really didn't love me; he loved the idea of being married to me. I don't feel like I lost a husband, but I lost a friend, and that feels just as bad."

"Annie I understand how you feel. Since your marriage to J.T., he and I didn't talk much, and when we did, it was only about maintaining the airplane, but now that he's gone I can't keep from thinking about the good days we once had together."

"Do you think he made a mistake? I hate to think he caused the death of his passenger."

"Let's wait for the NTSB report. They may sort it out."

Annie started to cry again. Brett got up, kissed Annie's forehead and said, "Will you sit with me while I have some dinner?"

"Sure," she replied as she dabbed her eyes with a Kleenex.

Brett set two places at the table in the kitchen nook, arranged the cardboard cartons and put a set of chopsticks next to each plate. He then went to the bar and poured a couple shots of Tanqueray into a metal shaker with ice, followed by two drops of vermouth. After vigorously shaking the mixture, he filled two martini glasses with the liquid and placed some olives on a saucer.

"Annie, come on in, I need company."

Annie joined him in the kitchen and slouched into a chair in the nook.

Brett set one of the martinis in front of her. "Tanqueray up, dry, and the olives on the side. Do you remember why we used to order them that way?"

A genuine smile creased Annie's lips. "Sure, we didn't want the olives in the glass to displace the gin. We got more alcohol with the olives on the side."

Brett held his glass up to Annie. She tapped hers against it and they both sipped the gin. "Open those cartons I'm starved." Annie said.

They passed the cartons back and forth using the chopsticks to spoon the food onto their plates. Brett started shoveling the food into his mouth, but most of it was falling back on his plate.

Annie started to laugh. "How can a terrific dentist like you who has such great hands, have so much trouble with chopsticks?"

Brett managed to grab a hold of a couple snow peas with his sticks. "I can only work with instruments when someone is drooling on them."

Annie had another laugh and thought how nice it was to share a meal with Brett again.

Brett knew in order to fight her depression, Annie had to get out and be with people. "I know you had been working at Nordstrom. Have you thought about going back?"

"Right now I just don't feel like sucking up to all those women whose biggest problem in life is what color shoes to wear with an outfit."

Brett picked up the shaker and began pouring the remainder of the martini into each glass. Annie waved him off and he poured it all into his. "We're purging the files in the office that are over seven years old, trying to get them into the storage room next door. Janet and Laurie have been trying to do it in between patients, but it's taking them forever. How would you like to help? It pays big time, seven-fifty an hour."

"Brett, you don't really need me. What do you think the women in the office are going to say when they see your ex working there?"

"Are you kidding? They ask about you all the time. After the divorce most of them were pretty upset with me because they lost you. They would jump at the chance to see you again on a regular basis."

Annie's smiled, but Brett could tell she was on the brink of tears. "I'll think about it," she said.

After the last nut was picked from the Cashew Chicken, Brett said to Annie, "If you'll clean up this mess of cartons, I'll go into J.T.'s office and see if I can dig up some more financial information for you."

Annie was feeling better. "That would be great, after I clean up, I'll be listening to music in the living room. Let me know what you find."

Brett sat down in the same leather chair in

which J.T. had sat when he presented them with their financial plan. He decided to look through the personal files first. A folder labeled PENINSULA MORTGAGE caught his eye.

On the top of the file were loan documents for a re-finance of the Atherton house. A year ago, in March of 1999, J.T. had obtained a new loan on the property in the amount of $2.4 million. After paying off the original $400,000 loan, J.T. pulled out two million in cash. The last year had brought a downturn in the real estate market and Brett figured the house was probably only worth about two million, leaving it $400,000 under water. The loan was written for thirty years at 7%, creating a payment of $15,967.26 a month. There were also four months of delinquent notices showing a past due balance of $63,869.04, plus late fees of $1,277.36.

Brett scrounged through the drawers of the desk and found J.T.'s check registers for 1999. He flipped to March and April. In March J.T. had made a deposit for $2 million. In April he had written a check to Sand Hill Venture Capital for exactly the same amount, $2 million. The note in the register said one million shares of MobileCom.

Brett was shocked. He remembered when J.T. had offered him the opportunity to invest in MobileCom, but it was way too risky for him and he had declined. A year later, when the dot-com bubble started to burst, MobileCom went belly up leaving the investors with nothing. Apparently

J.T. had lost all the money he had borrowed.

Brett opened the top drawer of the business file cabinet. All the client files were set neatly in alphabetical order except for two, which were sticking out in front of the A's. One was for Tony Russo, the client who died in the crash with J.T., and the other was for Claude Jennings, a name unfamiliar to Brett.

He opened the file for Tony Russo. His address was in Minneapolis. The papers on the top were copies of a life insurance policy purchased from J.T. six months ago. It was on Tony's life for $4.25 million listing the beneficiary as his wife, Maria Russo. At the bottom of the file was a ten year old letter dated September 27, 1990 from Tony to J.T. with a return address in New York City.

> Dear J.T.
>
> As you know I hold dual citizenship in both the U.S. and Italy. I finally got tired of the rat race and pressure filled life in New York. My family is still in Italy and I'm headed back there for what I hope will be a permanent stay.
>
> Thanks for all the good work you have done for me over the last five years. If you ever get to Italy, look me up. I'll be in the town of Fiesole where my family lives. It overlooks Florence.
>
> Best Regards.
> Tony

"That's strange," Brett mumbled to himself. Why would Tony Russo return to the U.S. after a ten year absence, and why was he on that fateful trip to Baja?

He opened up the file labeled Claude Jennings. It was obvious that J.T. had helped him with some investments which had provided a few nice commissions for J.T. In the middle of the folder were two slips of paper that looked as if they had been crumpled up, thrown away, and later retrieved. Brett gasped as he read them. The first note was unmistakably in J.T.'s handwriting.

Big money....Baja / Airplane
Cornea 20K
Kidney 25k
Pancreas 40K
Lung 40K
Heart 50K
200 K a shipment ??

The second note appeared to be written from Claude to J.T.

Okay Asshole !
You don't give me any choice
I'll help you with the deal in
Mex. but I think you're in way
over your head.
If you end up in the slammer,
you better not give me up.

*That would be very dangerous
to your health.*
C.

Brett was shaken by the discoveries he had just made. Had J.T. been desperate enough to get involved in some sort of illegal activity in Baja? As much as he didn't want to believe it, the notes were incriminating.

There was no denying that J.T. had lost two million dollars of borrowed money. He had also been behind in his mortgage payments and they were piling up at a rate of over $16,000 a month. It certainly appeared that J.T. had coerced this guy Claude Jennings into helping him with a shady deal down in Baja, and Brett couldn't help but wonder if the fiery crash had burned up a load of expensive contraband. The biggest question in his mind however, which made the hair on the back of his neck stand up, was whether the crash was an accident or the result of, as Claude Jennings had put it, "in way over your head."

He went back to the check book and noted down J.T.'s other major expenses.

Brett wrote down the addresses and phone numbers for Russo and Jennings on the back of the notes and stuffed them into his pants pocket. He wouldn't share any of this information with Annie; however, he had to let her know about the mortgage on the house and the other expenses.

Annie was listening to John Denver, when Brett joined her on the couch. Annie looked up and read the look on Brett's face. "Are you alright?"

"I'm fine. It's just a surprise to see what bad shape J.T. was in financially."

"How bad exactly?'

"Annie, is the house in J.T.'s name or is it community property?"

"It was always in his name, he never shared ownership with me. He kept it as his separate property. Why, is something wrong?"

Brett wasn't sure how to soften the news, so he just came out with it. "J.T. was way overextended. He owed almost two and half million dollars on the house. Your name isn't on the mortgage or the deed, so you won't have to pay it off, but the bank is going to take it back, eventually."

Brett expected Annie to break down but she looked unfazed. "I'm not surprised, I knew he was having financial problems; I just didn't realize they were that bad. I really don't mind moving out of this house; it never had any of me in it anyway. Everything in it was picked out and paid for by J.T. before I even moved in. Sometimes I felt like a guest here. The townhouse will always be the house that I remember as home. I'm so glad you never sold it."

Brett felt heartsick for Annie. "Let's not worry about it right now; it will probably be six months before the bank does anything, we'll figure it out then. You should get the insurance payment soon anyway, so there will be plenty of money for a new place."

Annie remained stoic as Brett continued. "There are some other big monthly bills that J.T. had. There's $1,200 a month for the plane and $700 a month for the lease on the new BMW. The plane costs are in limbo for awhile, so you won't have to be concerned. I'll turn the BMW back into the dealer for you. They'll probably want a couple thousand for breaking the lease, but you'll get rid of that payment. Unfortunately there are five credit card bills totaling about $190,000. Even though J.T. ran them up, it's a community property debt and as his wife you're still responsible for them. You're going to have to pay those and you'll still have all the costs that go along with running the house, about fifteen hundred a month. Do you need any cash to cover them for awhile?"

"Thanks, no, I have some money."

Annie got up to walk Brett to the door. Brett turned and put his arms around Annie's waist. "Give me hug."

Annie responded with a big squeeze.

"You're going to be alright." Brett said as he walked toward his car.

Annie was closing her front door, when Brett yelled back to her from the car. "Annie, nine a.m. sharp. Don't be late."

Chapter Six

Brett poured himself a snifter of brandy and headed straight up the stairs to his bedroom. He adjusted the temperature for above normal heat and turned on the water to the tub. While it was filling he undressed and threw his clothes into a pile in the corner near the gas fireplace. He took a sip of brandy as he turned off the water, started the whirlpool, and submerged himself up to his neck in the bubbling water. He was exhausted.

A week ago after the funeral, Annie's mom had asked Brett, "What ever happened between you and Annie? I had never seen two people more in love." He closed his eyes as he thought back to 1994.

He was at the chair telling one of his many stories to a patient. Ginger appeared at the entrance to the treatment room and held up a note.

YOUR WIFE IS ON THE PHONE.
Brett excused himself for a moment and slipped into his office to take the call.

"How did it go at the doctor's office?"

"Okay I guess." Annie sounded disappointed.

"What do you mean okay?"

Annie broke into hysterical laughter. "I'm pregnant. The baby is due in September."

"Oh Annie, I'm so happy. Why did you scare me so?"

"I'm sorry honey; I can't wait for you to get home."

"I'll be there in an hour. Call your mom."

The next few weeks were occupied with picking names and refurnishing the extra bedroom for the baby.

Annie had been driving a Honda Accord which really wasn't big enough for hauling around strollers and portable cribs. On Friday, Brett's day off, he said to Annie at breakfast. "Could you take my Porsche this morning? I need your Accord to move some parts at the airport."

"Okay, in a couple months I won't even be able to fit in the Porsche. This may be the last time I get to drive it for awhile."

"Great, I'll meet you back here for lunch."

At eleven forty-five Brett pushed the garage door opener and drove the car into the garage. He went into the house and yelled, "Hey Annie, I think something is wrong with the Honda. Take a look."

Annie came out from the kitchen. "What's wrong with it?"

"You tell me."

Annie opened the door to the garage and there sat a brand new Ford Explorer. "Oh my gosh, we have a family car." She gave him a hug. "Thanks hon."

A month later Annie opened the mailbox and there was a package from the Department of Motor Vehicles. She ripped off the paper and discovered a set of personalized license plates. 4MYBAYB.

Annie was having some morning sickness and several bouts with cramps, but managed to get through the first trimester with no apparent problems.

Brett announced at dinner one evening that J.T. had talked him into flying up to Yolo County Airport near Sacramento next Friday for a day of sky diving.

"Of what?" Annie exclaimed. "You don't know how to sky dive."

"I know, I know. It's not what you think. We're locked together with an instructor and he does all the work. All we do is go along for the ride. We'll make one jump in the morning and another after lunch. Hey, why don't you come along and watch?"

Annie hesitated. "I'll try, but it would be more fun if I were jumping with you guys."

On Friday Brett got up at six-thirty and turned on the coffee maker. Annie came down in her robe and Brett poured two cups. "What do think, wanna come along?"

Annie looked a little tired. "I don't think so, I was awake a lot last night with cramps. You go ahead; we can go out for dinner when you get home."

The flight from San Carlos to Yolo County only took twenty minutes. J.T. and Brett tied down the Baron and went into the terminal to register for the program. They were given jump suits and told that in a half hour there would be a briefing prior to the jumps. They each signed a disclaimer which made them wonder if this could actually be dangerous.

After the briefing, four students and four instructors piled into the back seats of an old Cessna 207, a workhorse airplane, which had been converted for jumping by the removal of its back doors. The pilot circled up to twelve thousand feet and everybody was ready for action. Brett felt butterflies in his stomach and J.T. remembered what it was like before a big football game.

They jumped two at a time, letting themselves free fall for about eight thousand feet. It was exhilarating; Brett felt like bird gliding through the air with only the sound of the wind passing by him. At four thousand feet the instructor opened the chute and there was a jolt as the fabric caught the air. They floated down and made a perfect landing with the instructor doing all the work.

Both Brett and J.T. were excited. They bought a sandwich and a coke and sat down to get ready for the afternoon jump. Brett retrieved his cell phone from his backpack and gave Annie a call. The machine picked up.

"Did you get a hold of her?" J.T. asked.

"No, she must be out or taking a nap. I'll call her after the next jump."

The afternoon jump appeared to be a carbon copy of the morning one with the absence of the apprehension they had felt earlier. J.T. and his instructor went first. Brett and his partner were second out of the plane and again his heart pounded rapidly from excitement.

Brett and his instructor landed about thirty yards from the runway and they could see commotion on the runway itself. Brett recognized J.T.'s chute lying on the ground and he ripped himself free of his straps and raced toward the crowd. J.T. was laying on the blacktop, bleeding from his chin and somewhat dazed.

"What happened?" Brett yelled to one of the bystanders.

"The student lost his footing on the landing and went chin first against the Tarmac."

Brett made his way through the crowd. "J.T., are you all right?"

J.T. tried to speak but his mouth wouldn't work.

Brett bent over him to survey his injuries. The skin on his chin was gone and it was bleeding badly, but that's not what caught Brett's attention. He could see swelling in front of J.T.'s right ear. He gently palpated the joint that connects the lower mandible to the maxilla. Brett was very familiar with the anatomy of the temporomandibular joint. The lower jaw, the mandible, fits up into a depression in the temporal bone of the skull. It's held in place by muscles and ligaments, which allow it to articulate open and closed.

His fingers gingerly felt the upper part of the condyle, the section of the mandible closest to the temporal bone. He could feel the fracture immediately. The condyle had separated from the body of the mandible, the reason J.T. couldn't open his mouth to speak. Brett remembered that boxers were prone to this type of fracture. They would get hit in the chin, which would drive the lower jaw into the bone of the skull.

Brett called for a first aid kit, ice and an Ace bandage. He placed the bandage under J.T.'s chin and wound it over the top of his head. He repeated the rotation three times and taped the edges together. This immediately stabilized the jaw and J.T. was able to squeeze a few words out through closed teeth.

"Goo goin doc, et's get da ell ot of ere."

"Hang in there J.T. I've got a few more things to take care of."

Brett placed the ice over the fracture and asked J.T. to hold it in place. Then he washed J.T.'s chin with a wipe from the kit, covered it with Neosporin, and taped a 4x4 gauze over the wound. "I need a glass of water and a straw." Brett ordered. An employee had it there in about ninety seconds.

Brett took four Ibuprofen tablets out of the first aid kit, put them inside a gauze pad and smashed them up with the tin box. Then he dumped the powder into the water and stirred it up with the straw. He placed the straw in between J.T.'s lips. "Suck all this up. You're really going to need it."

Brett retrieved his cell phone from his backpack. He dialed the number of the oral surgeon whose office was next door to his. The receptionist answered.

Brett didn't want to alarm her, but he sternly said, "Joanne, this is Dr. Raven, I have to speak with Dr. James right away, it's urgent."

There was a click in the phone. "Brett what's so important?"

"Dick, my buddy just fractured his jaw in an accident up near Sacramento. I'm going to get him in the plane and get him back as soon as I can."

"How long will it take to get him to Sequoia Hospital?"

Brett looked at his watch. It was almost three o'clock. "I should have him there by four."

"I'll meet you in the emergency room." He clicked off.

J.T. was able to walk to the plane while still holding the ice to the right side of his face. Brett opened the double back doors and let him spread out over two of the seats. He managed to get a lap belt around him, and then closed the doors. Brett fired up the engines and was in the air in five minutes.

They arrived at the emergency entrance at ten minutes after four. Dick James was already there; he immediately examined the injury and ordered x-rays. When the x-rays were delivered, he spoke to J.T. "Brett was right. You fractured the condyle of your right mandible. We're going to prep you for surgery. I'll go in there, re-align the condyle with the body of the mandible and put a small plate with a couple screws in to hold it in place. I'm going to have to wire your upper and lower teeth together so there's no movement in that joint for awhile. I'm afraid you'll be on a liquid diet for about six weeks."

J.T. couldn't speak so he put his right thumb in the air.

Brett said, "Good luck J.T., I'll see you in a couple hours."

Dealing with the injury to J.T. had caused Brett to completely forget he hadn't talked to Annie all day. He dialed the house and got the answering machine again.

"This isn't like Annie." He ran to his car.

Annie's car was in the garage. Brett came crashing into the house through the door from the garage. "Annie, Annie, where are you?" There was no response, just a light coming from the kitchen. Brett rushed toward it. "Oh my God,

Annie."

Annie was on her back, spread out on the floor with the phone receiver lying next to her. The pants of her beige warm ups were stained solid red from just below her waist to just above her knees, and there was a small pool of blood next to her buttocks.

Brett shook her lightly. "Annie, Annie can you hear me?" Annie groaned. Brett grabbed the receiver, pushed the green button and dialed 911. "I need an ambulance right away. My wife is bleeding from the vagina and she's unconscious. We're at 44 Geranium Lane in San Carlos."

Annie was pale and very clammy feeling. Brett pulled the afghan off the couch and covered her with it. He laid down next to her and put his arms around her.

Brett followed the ambulance to the emergency room at Sequoia Hospital. For the second time today, he rushed through the sliding glass doors

The nurses took Annie into a treatment room, checked her vital signs, placed oxygen over her nose and hooked her up to an IV with a glucose drip.

"Is she going to be alright?" Brett asked the head nurse.

"She's lost a lot of blood, but her vitals are pretty good. She's starting to come around and she's mumbling a few words. Our ER doctor has called her OB."

Brett held Annie's hand until her doctor

arrived. She kept mumbling the same words over and over again. "Brett, where are you, Brett where are you?"

Brett was sick to his stomach with guilt and fear. He ran down the corridor to the men's room and vomited into the toilet.

Annie's doctor acknowledged Brett as he went into her treatment room. When he came out, he motioned to Brett. "As soon as we get some fluids in her, we'll move her to the O.R. There's no hope for the baby, my main concern right now is for her uterus, there may be some permanent damage."

Annie was in the operating room for an hour an a half. Her doctor, dressed in green scrubs, entered the waiting room and sat down next to Brett. "Her uterus didn't look very good."

"What does that mean?" Brett asked while holding back tears.

"She'll recover just fine, but I have to tell you Brett, I don't think she should ever get pregnant again."

Brett was shocked. "Why?"

"Has Annie ever had a D&C.?"

Brett went pale and had to sit down.

"Are you okay?" The doctor inquired.

"I have to tell you, Annie had an abortion fourteen years ago. Every couple years she's had bleeding and at least three D&C's to stop it."

The doctor sat down next to him. "Here's the deal. We think Annie has a condition called Asherman's Syndrome. Ever hear of it?"

"Never."

"I'm not surprised. Asherman's Syndrome occurs in a small percentage of women after having D&C procedures. It's actually scarring of the uterus accompanied with fibrosis and adhesions. It's impossible to carry a fetus in a uterus with that kind of scarring, that's why she had this miscarriage"

"Are, are you telling me that Annie will never be able to have a baby?"

This was the conversation which all doctors dread. "Brett, I'm actually worried that some of the muscles of the uterus have been damaged. If Annie gets pregnant again, there could be a risk of uterine rupture. That could threaten her life."

"What if I had gotten her to the hospital earlier? Could any of this have been prevented?"

"Brett, I don't know when the damage was done. Maybe during the abortion or maybe after one of the D&C's, but there's nothing you could have done to prevent this miscarriage."

Brett couldn't see Annie until she was moved back into her room. He was let in after the doctor had spent forty-minutes with her and, when he entered, she was crying. He bent down to kiss her cheek, but she put her hand between them. "I can't talk to you right now, I just can't."

This was not the time to bring forth any explanations. All Brett could say was, "Annie, I'm so sorry."

Both J.T. and Annie went home from the hospital

on Monday. J.T. took a cab and Brett picked up Annie. Annie's doctor was at the hospital and he motioned Brett aside. "I'm giving you a couple names of psychologists. I think Annie is going to need some help." On the ride home Brett tried to start a conversation, but he couldn't get any response from Annie.

When they arrived home, Annie told Brett she wanted time alone. She asked him to take out the baby furniture and bring back the queen bed so he could sleep in that room.

Brett tried to get Annie to talk, but she remained almost mute until one evening at the dinner table she erupted. "He would have been fifteen last Friday."

"Who?"

Annie's anger was unleashed. "Our child, that's who! The one we let get sucked down a tube."

"Annie we decided.."

"You mean you decided. I waited as long as I could; still hoping you would change your mind. All you said was 'it's not like you'll never get pregnant again. We can still have those kids we talked about'."

Annie picked up her plate and threw it at Brett. "How does that sound now?"

He watched the spaghetti drip off the wall. "We can still adopt."

Annie got up from the table and started upstairs. "You just don't get it, you never did. I wanted a baby of my own." She went in her room and slammed the door.

Brett tried to talk to Annie a couple days later. "Let's see a psychologist together. We can work through this."

"I don't want to work through it; I'm in mourning and you should be too."

Brett had no defense. Ten years ago he had promised to make up for the sacrifices Annie had made, and now he knew he could never keep his promise.

Annie hadn't talked to Brett in five days, when she approached him. "I think it would be best if you found yourself an apartment."

"Annie I love you, I want to be with you."

Annie remained detached. "I think it would be best if you found yourself an apartment."

Tears came to Brett's eyes. "Please Annie, don't do this. What about all our dreams?"

She said without emotion. "We lost those, when we lost our babies."

Brett found a place to live not far from his office and began his life away from his college sweetheart. Six weeks later, a man walked into Brett's office, asked if he was Dr. Brett Raven, and served him with divorce papers.

Brett appeared at the attorney's office for a property settlement with Annie. They each kept their cars, they split the cash and investments, Annie kept the townhouse, and Brett kept his practice and his partnership in the airplane. Brett agreed to pay Annie $4,000 a month for the next five years.

Brett asked J.T. to meet him for a drink after work at the British Bankers Club. He looked at the scar on J.T.'s cheek. "How's the jaw doing?"

"Its fine, but I guarantee I'll never jump out of an airplane again."

Brett smiled and brought up the subject he really wanted to discuss. "J.T., I'm worried about Annie. Would you start dropping in on her? See if you can persuade her to get some therapy?"

"Do you think she'll listen to me?"

"Annie's very fond of you. She's always had a great respect for your intellect. The fact that you're taller than I and better looking helps a little also."

J.T. smiled. "Sure, I'll give it a try."

Brett didn't talk to Annie at all during the next six months; however, he would get progress reports from J.T. Apparently, Annie was seeing a psychologist and her depression was lessening. J.T. was making an effort to be with her whenever he wasn't traveling on business.

J.T. called Brett and asked if they could meet for a drink at the BBC.

J.T looked nervous. "What's up, we having problems with the plane?" Brett asked.

J.T. wouldn't make eye contact. "This is really difficult Brett. You and I have been best friends and I find myself in an awkward position."

Brett sensed what was coming. "It's you and Annie, isn't it?"

"Brett, I feel like a traitor to you, I never dreamed this would happen. I tried to stop it, but I couldn't. We're talking about getting married."

Brett couldn't speak and felt a flush of heat rising through his neck. "Say that again."

"I'm sorry, really sorry, I can't explain it. It just happened."

Brett got off his stool and kicked it upside down. He shoved his face up to J.T. "You piece of shit. I asked you to look after her, not get into her pants."

J.T. still wouldn't look Brett in the eye. "You got it wrong. I wasn't interested in that. I just love being with her."

"All the fuckin' women clinging to you and you go after my ex-wife."

"She needs me."

"She's vulnerable and needs support, not a bed partner."

J.T. regained his composure. "We set a date six weeks from Saturday. She wants to talk to you."

Brett kicked the toppled bar stool and headed for the door. "Don't expect a wedding present." He said as he let the door slam behind him.

Brett called Annie the next day, and she asked if he could stop by the townhouse for a talk. It felt strange knocking on the door of the house he and Annie had picked out together. She answered the knock and invited him into the living room.

Brett sat on the couch, Annie on the stuffed chair. Annie started the conversation. "Brett, I think you know I'm in therapy."

"I heard that. How's it going?"

"Pretty good, the depression is almost gone and a lot of my anger has disappeared."

"I'm glad."

Annie broke eye contact and looked down at the floor. "Brett, I know this is hard for you."

Brett sat silent.

"I'd like to say I'm sorry, but this time I have to do what feels right for me."

"Annie, do you know what you're doing? J.T. has been our best friend, but you know how slick he is. You just don't fit with him."

Annie just gave a weak smile. "Brett, after the wedding I'll be moving into J.T.'s house. I want you to take the townhouse."

"Annie, the townhouse is yours. You can sell it or rent it out."

Annie made eye contact again. "You don't understand, I don't want a stranger living in this house. This house was for you and me. We've lived in it together, I've lived in it by myself, and now it's your turn."

"Annie, I appreciate it, but this house is worth a lot of money, I wouldn't feel right."

Annie picked up an envelope off the coffee table. "Well you don't have any choice. This is the deed to the house. I had the attorney put it in your name this morning."

Annie walked Brett to the door. They shook hands and Brett said, "Thanks Annie, I really hope you know what you're doing."

Neither Brett nor J.T. would let go of half the Baron. They worked out a formula whereby every other week the use of plane would alternate between them. The maintenance was turned over to a local aircraft management group, which eliminated any need for meetings.

Brett had no communication with either J.T or Annie for almost a year, until on September fifteenth, his birthday, a card arrived at his office.

B.

I still remember the good
times. Be well.

A.

Brett called Annie that afternoon. "Hi Annie, its Brett."

"Oh Brett, happy birthday."

"Thanks, I got the card this morning. It was sweet."

"How have you been?"

"Fine, you?"

"I'm good. I broke free of therapy six weeks ago, and I took a job at Nordstrom in the Women's Active department"

"That's great."

Annie felt the awkwardness of the conversation and changed the subject. "How's the townhouse, any changes?"

"Pretty much the same except for less food in

the fridge."

Annie felt a twinge of guilt and pity. "Are you cooking?"

"Sometimes." There was a long silence. "Hey, I just wanted to thank you for the card, I have to get back to a patient."

"It was nice to hear your voice."

"Yours too," Brett replied as he hung up.

Every year a card arrived on his birthday with the same message.

B.

**I still remember the good
times. Be well.**

A.

Brett would always follow up with a phone call.

One day in early December of 1999, Ginger signaled Brett that he had a phone call. He slipped out of the treatment room and asked. "Who is it?"

"You won't believe it, but it's J.T. Talbot"

"What the hell does he want?"

"I have no idea, but he said it's important."

Brett went to his private office, picked up the receiver, and pushed the lighted button. "Hello J.T., is anything wrong with Annie?"

"No, Brett, she fine. It's something else."

"What's so important, that you would call me after four years?"

"I apologize, but do you remember that company DKL Pharmaceuticals?"

"The one we bought at ten dollars and went to seventy?"

"Yeah that's it, do you still own it?"

Brett was very proud of that investment. He had invested fifty thousand dollars and the stock was now worth three hundred and fifty thousand. "Definitely, it's over one half of my retirement fund."

"Brett I realize I'm no longer your financial advisor, but I had to call you. Get rid of the stock today."

A bead of sweat erupted on Brett's upper lip. "Why, what's happening?"

"We found that stock because I knew a mole in the company who let us in early. Well, he just called me. Their biggest drug, Prodantin, is being pulled off the market tomorrow. Some research guy linked it to at least a thousand deaths. I'm not sure the company can survive the fallout."

Now Brett's hand began to tremble. "How do I get out?"

"I still have a securities license; I can sell it for you. Brett, I don't want any commission, I just want to get you out."

"I have the certificates in my safe deposit box."

"Cancel a patient and go get them. I can pick them up from you; however, we have to get them sold before the New York exchange closes at one o'clock our time.

Brett followed J.T.'s instructions and the stock was sold at twelve fifty-five Pacific time.

J.T. dropped a check at Brett's office for three hundred and forty-eight thousand dollars at three o'clock that afternoon. The next morning the business section of the Chronicle ran a lead story: THE COLLAPSE OF DKL PHARMACEUTICALS

Brett called J.T. "I don't know what to say except, thanks."

"Brett, Annie never would have forgiven me if I hadn't called."

"Well, it was still you who threw me the life line. I owe you, thanks again."

"Brett, you don't owe me. Fly safe, partner."

That was the last time Brett talked to J.T.

Part II

Confusion

Chapter Seven

The last time Brett had talked to J.T. was to thank him for the rescue from financial disaster. Now he felt an obligation to repay the debt and to discover what had befallen J.T. on that last flight from Baja.

He looked at his patient schedule for the day. There was a cancellation from eleven to twelve and combined with his lunch break, he had a couple hours of free time. He examined the notes he had found in Claude Jennings file on which he had scribbled Claude's address and phone number.

Brett dialed the phone number and a raspy voice answered. "Jennings."

"Mr. Jennings, my name is Brett Raven. I was a friend of J.T. Talbot and I'm helping with the closure of his client files. Could I stop by your office and tie up some loose ends?"

The phone was silent for about ten

seconds. "What loose ends?"

"If you can spare about ten minutes, I'll stop by your office and fill you in."

Jennings sounded irritated but said, "Okay, I'll be here for about an hour." He hung up.

Brett checked the address for Claude Jennings Imports—1257A El Camino Real in San Mateo. He had to drive around the block three times before he finally located it, because the entrance wasn't readily visible from the street. Visitors had to walk into an alcove and climb a flight of stairs leading to a door with no identification other than the letter 'A'.

Brett tried the door, it was locked. He knocked twice and waited for a response. The door opened and Brett said, "Mr. Jennings, I'm Brett Raven, J.T. Talbot's friend. I called you earlier this morning?"

"Oh yeah, terrible, terrible about J.T. Come on in."

Claude didn't fit the image Brett had pictured in his mind. Claude was about fifty years old, but was probably taken for sixty with his bald head and pot belly. His face was puffy and his nose was a reddish color, giving Brett the impression that he drank too much. It looked as if he had shaved that morning but had missed the entire section under his chin, where stubble was still visible. He wore an old pair of khakis that were un-pressed and a sport shirt which was decorated with a piece of the scrambled egg he apparently had eaten for breakfast.

Claude led him to a chair in front of an old desk,

which looked like it had been purchased from the Salvation Army thirty years earlier.

"Nasty, very nasty." Claude said as he took a seat behind the desk. "I read about it in the newspaper. What happened, did he run out of gas?"

"I doubt it; he was too experienced. The fire was horrendous; it takes a lot of gas to fuel one that hot."

Brett glanced at the wall behind Claude which displayed about a half dozen photos of him in different settings. The first one that caught his eye was of Claude standing next to a high winged airplane. Brett recognized it as a Cessna 206, commonly known as a Stationair. It was one of the largest of the high wing Cessna's and employed a powerful 300 HP engine up front. It was commonly used to haul heavy loads and had a large clamshell rear door to assist with loading. The registration number on the plane was N206CJ. It was obvious it stood for the type of the plane and the initials of its owner.

"Is that your 206?" Brett inquired.

Claude glanced behind him. "Yeah, I've had it for about ten years."

Brett was surprised. "I had no idea you were a pilot; J.T. never mentioned you. I owned the Baron with him."

"That must be tough. You not only lost your buddy, but you also lost a beautiful bird."

"The insurance will replace the plane, but nothing will bring J.T. back. Did you ever get a chance to fly with him?"

Claude didn't answer. Instead he picked a used toothpick off his desk and began working the last of his breakfast from his front teeth. Finally he said, "Well, we talked about it but, it never seemed to happen."

"How did you meet J.T. anyway?" Brett inquired.

"My business started to turn a few bucks a couple years ago. I had a little cash and needed some help managing it, so I went to one of J.T.'s seminars."

"That's interesting; I met him the same way. He was a pretty impressive guy. By the way, what exactly is your business?"

Claude was getting a little uneasy. He wasn't comfortable answering questions about his business. "I import artifacts mainly."

"Really! Where does one find artifacts these days?"

Claude reached into his top drawer and pulled out a cigar. He bit off the end, spit it on the floor, and then lit it with a lighter he picked off the desk. "Mind if I smoke?"

Brett couldn't stand smoking and cigars were especially repugnant. "No, go right ahead."

"I usually get the merchandise from Mexico. That's what I use the plane for."

"Who buys them from you? I've never seen an artifact store."

Claude blew out a puff of smoke. It lingered in

the air and then settled down in Brett's immediate proximity. He pretended to ignore it, knowing that all his clothes would be headed to the cleaners as soon as he left. "Oh, I have a couple regular wholesalers who take them off my hands."

Brett got up off his chair and walked to the wall with the pictures. The one next to the 206 showed Claude, who was only about five foot six, flanked on either side by two men, both at least six feet tall, dark complected, and sporting black moustaches. The one on the right was dressed in a uniform. "This is an interesting picture. Where was it taken?" Brett asked.

"Mexico, down in Baja."

"Who's the general?"

"He isn't military. His name is Jorge Rivera and he's the police chief of Cabo San Lucas. The guy on the left is his brother Miguel. He's a big time doctor down there."

"Looks like you're good friends."

Claude smiled for the first time. "Let's just say that Jorge helps me with the exporting of the artifacts out of Mexico. Miguel is a collector and finds the products for me."

Brett strolled back to his chair. He was getting ready to drop the bomb, and he wanted to frame his words just right. "Did you and J.T. ever partner in any business deals?"

Claude's demeanor immediately changed; his face became blank and his eyes turned into little slits. "Why the hell would you think that?"

Brett could feel a little sweat forming under his armpits. "As a favor to his widow, I took on the job of going through J.T.'s personal stuff and I came across your name several times."

"Really, I can't imagine why J.T. would have my name in his personal records. What exactly did it pertain to?"

Here it comes Brett thought to himself. "It looked to me like he was in the import business with you."

"Why would J.T. want to be in the import business?"

"J.T. was getting a little short of money. I hear there's a lot of it dealing with artifacts."

Claude forced a laugh. "Look around, does it look like I'm making a lot of dough?"

"Looks can be deceiving. Exactly how much does an artifact that looks like a heart or kidney bring on the wholesale market?"

Claude stared at Brett. Brett stared back. He knew the first to speak was going to lose the standoff. Finally Claude broke the silence. "You know, Raven, it was nice talking to you. My condolences to J.T.'s widow. Stay in touch." He got up and opened the door.

Brett slipped into his blue Porsche coupe, a vintage 356C model built in 1965. Annie had insisted they make payments on it as a graduation present to him and he hadn't put up much of a fight.

He reached under the folded back seat, pulled out his 35mm Nikon and slouched down as far as could. He didn't have long to wait; within five minutes Claude came scurrying out of the alcove. Brett zoomed in, put the shutter on the rapid setting, and clicked off a half dozen close ups of Claude's face.

When Brett got back to his townhouse, he went immediately to his office and powered up his iMac. He clicked the AOL icon and put in his password, 2THDOC. It took a few minutes but he finally found the website www.findafriend.com. He registered on the home page and paid the $9.95 fee with his Visa card. Brett typed in the name, MIGUEL RIVERA M.D. Five names came up, however, only one had a residence in Mexico. He clicked the name.

<u>Miguel Rivera M.D.</u>
<u>Education</u>
B.S.	**University of Texas**
M.D.	**University of Southern California Medical School**
Pathology	**Harbor General Hospital, Los Angeles, Ca.**

<u>Special achievements</u>
Expert in the field of Cryonics
<u>Employment</u>
Coroner	**Baja del Sur, Mexico**

Brett went back to the AOL homepage and placed a search for CRYONICS. A definition popped up;

Cryonics :
The emerging medical technology of cryopreserving. The use of very cold temperatures on human tissues and organs with the intention of future revival.

He returned to the search engine and typed in, ORGAN BLACK MARKET. Up came dozens of articles with names such as, <u>Organ Trafficking is no Myth</u>, <u>The Organ Black Market</u>, <u>Organ Shortage Fuels Illicit Trade In Human Parts</u>.

He spent an hour reading through the articles and then put the computer to sleep.

Chapter Eight

Brett was having trouble concentrating on his patients. He kept thinking about the information he had gleaned from the internet last night. He took a break and went into his private office.

Brett usually played tennis two or three times a week at the Pacific Athletic Club. He located his tennis roster and thumbed down to the name Michael Grossman M.D. He and Brett were doubles partners two years ago in the USTA 4.5 league.

Doctor Grossman's office phone number was listed and Brett dialed it. A fresh young voice answered. "Dr. Grossman's office."

"Hi, this is Dr. Raven; I wanted to speak to Dr. Grossman. It's a personal call."

"Hold on a minute Dr. Raven, he's standing right here next to the desk."

"Brett, I haven't heard from you in over a year. What's up?"

"Sorry, Mike, I haven't played any tennis for at least six months. Hey, I know you're a cardiovascular surgeon, are you doing any transplants?"

Dr. Grossman was a little surprised. "I am; I hope you don't need one."

Brett laughed. "No thanks, but I have a patient who has asked me to help him get some information. Any chance I could buy you lunch and pick your brain?"

"I never turn down a free lunch, how about tomorrow at the club, around twelve thirty?"

"See you there."

Brett arrived early and found a table. Mike Grossman joined him ten minutes later and Brett stood and shook his hand. "Good to see you again."

"You too, you're looking well. How's that menu?"

"It's pretty nice. If I were you I'd order one of the heart healthy items."

They laughed and ordered as soon as the waitress appeared. Brett got right down to business. "I have a patient who needs a heart transplant. He's way down on the list and it doesn't look like he can wait his turn. Apparently he's been contacted by the black market. He asked my opinion and I have no idea what he's talking about. Can you fill me in a little?"

"I sure can. First of all you have to understand

how organs are distributed to donors in the United States. There's an organization called the United Network for Organ Sharing. A potential recipient gets on that list you mentioned. Right now there's probably between fifty to seventy thousand people on the various organ waiting lists."

Brett was astonished. "Holy shit, no wonder people die before reaching the top of the list."

The waitress placed the sandwiches down on the table. Dr. Grossman paused with his presentation to take a couple bites from his chicken sandwich and went on. "Yeah, that's the reason there's a huge Black Market in organ trafficking. Worldwide it's a billion dollar a year industry."

Brett hadn't touched his food. He was fascinated with what he was hearing. "Do we have much of it here in the U.S.?" He asked.

"The hotbeds are in the Middle East and China. Poor people get paid $1,000 for a kidney and the marketeers sell it for $25,000 to $100,000. Most of them are sold locally and transplanted in hospitals right in those countries or very nearby."

Brett was into it. "Why don't they send them to the U.S.? We have the long waiting lists."

By now Dr. Grossman had finished his sandwich and was mopping a fry through his ketchup. Brett still hadn't taken a bite. "Some find their way here, but you have to remember, these organs are living tissues. There's a finite time after harvest to get them into a recipient."

Brett just remembered he was talking to a heart surgeon. "Wait a minute, how can someone sell their heart?"

"I was wondering when that question was going to come. Hearts, livers, pancreas, all come out of people, who have recently died. Marketeers can get a hold of some of these; however, kidneys are easier, because no one has to die to harvest one."

Now Brett was getting close to extracting the information he was after. "How are they transported?"

"There are companies around the world who are in the business of organ transport. Usually they are transported in a semi-frozen state, but there are new techniques, which actually pump blood through them to keep them alive."

Brett finally nibbled at his food. "My patient told me he was approached by a black market guy who told him he could get a heart preserved by cryonic methods. Is that for real or is it bullshit?"

Dr. Grossman had to think for a minute. "I've read there's a lot of research going on to preserve these organs indefinitely at sub zero temperatures, but to my knowledge the process hasn't been refined. I know that ethical doctors in the U.S. wouldn't touch them."

"Then how could he get the transplant?"

"Well, there are numerous private surgical centers operating in that gray zone between ethical and unethical."

Brett was ready for his final question. "If you

had a failing heart and knew you wouldn't reach the top of the list, would you take a chance on a cryonic preserved one?"

"You know Brett, if I had the money and a doctor to implant it, I'd have nothing to lose if it failed."

Brett picked up the check and put twenty dollars on the table. They walked out to the parking lot together

"Thanks for lunch," Dr. Grossman said.

"Thank you, Mike. You've been very informative, I'll pass it on. Let's play tennis soon."

Chapter Nine

Brett laid awake that night thinking about his conversation with Mike Grossman. Was it possible cryonic organs were being transplanted right here on the San Francisco Peninsula? He had an idea and jumped out of bed.

He opened his computer and went onto the internet. He remembered there was a new website that a guy had started out of his garage in San Francisco about four years ago and it was becoming very popular for all sorts of free advertising.

He typed www.craigslist.com into the address box and clicked. The website came to life. Brett scrolled through the categories listed on the home page. He stopped at one titled *Services* and opened the page. One of the sub categories was titled *Health & Wellness*. He clicked again and up came the first of twenty-six pages of various services.

One by one Brett surveyed each page. An hour

and eighteen pages later, he spotted an ad which interested him.

SAN FRANCISCO BAY AREA SURGICAL TRANSPLANT CENTER.
Contact us for organ transplant needs. Seniority on the transplant list is not a requirement. We have immediate access to transplant organs. 650-555-2727.

The next day during his morning break, he dialed the number from Craigslist, which was in same area code as his own. A young female voice answered. "Transplant Center, how may I help you?"

"Yes, I'm interested in finding out more about your services."

"I can help you. What are you looking for?"

"I've been told I need a heart transplant, and I'm several years down the waiting list. I visited your website and it implied you don't have a waiting list."

"That's true; we use a different approach to organ transplants. Our normal procedure is to make an appointment for you to come to our center where a counselor can give you a complete explanation of our services and also determine, if you would qualify for them. Can I make you an appointment?"

Brett hesitated for a moment; he hadn't expected to actually visit the center. "Yes, that would be fine."

The cheerful voice continued. "Wonderful, could I have your name?"

Brett decided to give his real name just in case he had to show some identification. "Brett Raven."

"One of our counselors could see you next Friday

at eleven thirty, Mr. Raven."

"Where exactly are you located? I'm on the peninsula in San Carlos."

"Oh that's perfect. We're in Menlo Park about five miles down the freeway."

It was too late for Brett to back out. "Next Friday would be fine." Brett hung up the receiver and opened the phonebook lying next to it. He found the address for a medical supply store in Belmont, the neighboring city to San Carlos.

On Friday morning Brett purposely did not shave or wash his hair. He wanted to look scruffy. He drove to the medical supply store and purchased a portable oxygen unit. It consisted of a small tank that was fitted on a rolling cart with a handle. There was a plastic line from the unit to a cannula, which fit under his nose and was held in place by an elastic strap behind his head. He also bought a cane.

Brett parked away from the building and unloaded the oxygen unit. He strapped on the cannula and pulled the unit with his left hand while placing the cane in his right. He entered the suite labeled Surgical Transplant Center.

The receptionist spotted Brett coming in. She jumped to her feet and came out to greet him. "Please sit here," she said as she pulled out a chair for him.

"Thank You." Brett said as he took deep breaths from his mouth. "My name is Brett Raven, I have an appointment with a counselor."

"Oh yes, Mr. Raven. Could I have you fill out a short information form and also get a copy of your driver's license? She handed him the form and said, "Mr. Shaw is waiting to see you. I'll tell him you're here."

The young woman returned and said, "Mr. Shaw can see you now. Please take your time, there's no hurry."

Brett rose to his feet and breathing deeply and slowly, shuffled into the office pulling the oxygen unit behind him as he leaned heavily on the cane. A man in his early fifties dressed in a blue suit came to greet him. "Good afternoon, Mr. Raven, I'm Chris Shaw. It's nice to meet you."

Brett leaned against a chair, rested his cane and gave Chris Shaw a wet fish handshake.

"Thank you for seeing me."

Mr. Shaw helped Brett into a chair and took a seat next to him. "So tell me Mr. Raven, what is your medical condition at this time?"

Brett tried to take deep breaths between words. "I have congestive heart failure. I've been told I need a transplant, but the doctors don't think I'll make it long enough to reach the top of the list."

Shaw replied in a sympathetic voice, "Unfortunately, we see this all too often. Let me explain our facility. We have a full surgical staff, which includes surgeons, anesthesiologists, and surgical nurses. We have a state of the art operating room and recovery center, where we maintain a six bed hospital for the recuperation phase of treatment."

Brett coughed several times into a handkerchief.

"I'm curious, Mr. Shaw, how can you get me a heart without a waiting list?"

"Please call me Chris. May I call you Brett?"

Brett nodded his head. "Brett, patients who come to us have to realize we are their last chance to stay alive. We don't guarantee success; however, we have favorable result numbers. As an answer to your question, we are able to obtain organs which have been removed from a deceased in another country and are frozen at sub zero temperatures before transporting them to us here in the U.S."

"Do they work?"

"Some do and some don't. That's why I say we can't guarantee success. With the transplant of a heart we have a twenty-eight percent success rate."

Brett curled his brow. "You mean seventy-two percent of the patients die?"

"Brett, keep in mind that a hundred percent of those patients would die anyway before reaching the top of the list. That makes a twenty-eight percent success rate look quite good."

Brett took another deep hit on his oxygen. "Is it legal to use frozen hearts?"

"We require you to sign several documents: a consent to use the frozen organ in your body, a document explaining the procedure may fail and death will occur, another document explaining this is an experimental procedure, and a consent to being part of a research project for the advancement of medicine. After you understand and sign these documents, the procedure is legal and ethical."

"I'm guessing you know what my next question is."

Chris smiled. "You want to know what the costs will be."

Brett nodded the affirmative.

"None of our services are covered by insurance. The costs are extraordinarily high; however, you will be paying for the most valuable commodity on earth—your life."

Chris stopped talking, let his words sink in, and then he continued. "The cost of the organ is $100,000. The fee for the surgery is $100,000. The cost for the recovery in our hospital is $10,000 per day."

"How many days will I need for recovery?"

"The minimum stay would be ten days; however, three weeks is the average."

Brett did the quick math in his head. "So, if I stayed for twenty-one days, I'd have a total cost of $410,000."

"That sounds about right."

"I guess poor people just make funeral arrangements."

"Unfortunately, this is not a social program. We do, however, have a third party lender who can help with the costs."

Brett raised an eyebrow. "How does that work?"

Chris went to his desk and took out a folder. He opened it and took out a sheet of paper. "If you have enough equity in your house, our lender will take a second mortgage against it and provide the funds for the procedure." He handed the sheet to Brett.

Brett looked over the financing for $400,000. The lender charges 12% interest. The loan calls for interest only payments for ten years at which time a balloon payment of $400,000 is due. "So it would cost me about $4,000 a month for ten years. If I can't come up with the money in ten years, I guess I lose the house."

Chris smiled. "Still better than the alternative."

Brett slowly got up on his feet, assembled his portable unit, and lifted his cane. "I'll have to discuss this with my wife."

Chris rose to help Brett toward the door. "I understand. As a favor Brett, because this is such an unconventional procedure, I'd appreciate, if you only share the information with your spouse."

"I'll be discreet. By the way, are you familiar with a man named Claude Jennings?

The smile on Chris's face disappeared for a second, and then he recovered with a grin. "Yes, Claude helps us once in awhile with transportation issues. Do you know him?"

"Yes, he was the one who suggested I look into your services."

Chris opened the door. "I'll have to remember to thank him. Good day Brett."

Chapter Ten

Annie received a registered letter from Connecticut Mutual Life. It was dated June 12, 2000, three months to the day after the crash of the Baron.

Dear Mrs. Talbot:

We received your request for payment on policy L275621 insuring the life of John Thomas Talbot. The death of Mr. Talbot has been confirmed and Connecticut Mutual Life has approved the payment of the death benefit. The value of the death benefit is $5,000,000. You may receive the payment by certified check or by direct wire transfer to a bank account. Please let us know which method you prefer. If you choose direct wire transfer, please supply us with the name of the bank, the account number and the routing number.

Our condolences for your loss.

Sincerely,

Ralph Cramer

Vice President

Policy Benefits

Annie was working at Brett's office the day after the letter arrived. She was in the lounge having a cup of coffee when Brett walked in. "How's the file purge project going?" Brett asked, as he added sweetener to a cup of black coffee.

"This is real work. I've been at it for a couple months and I'm only half way there. I may have to ask for a raise."

"No can do. If I give you a raise, I'll have to raise everybody in the office. I'm afraid you'll have to go to the union."

Annie laughed and said. "Okay, I'd hate to see picket signs in front of your office." Her smile disappeared and she became serious. "Brett, I received the notice from the insurance company yesterday. They want to know how to send me the payment, and I'm not sure what to do or where to put that amount of money. Would it be asking too much for you to help me?"

"Annie, it's not too much at all. How about dinner tonight and we'll discuss it. Pick you up at seven?"

Annie looked relieved. "That would be wonderful, casual, right?"

"Absolutely, but don't try to hit me up again for a raise. Seven seventy-five an hour has maxed me out."

Brett parked the Porsche in the driveway and knocked on the door. Annie opened it and said, "Come on in. Make yourself a drink, I'm almost ready."

Brett went to the bar and poured two fingers of scotch into an old fashion glass. He walked to the back window and looked out at the pool.

Annie snuck up behind him. "Penny for your thoughts."

"Oh, I didn't hear you come in." Brett turned around and smiled at Annie. She looked magnificent. Her hair was pushed back the way she always used to wear it. She had on a white silk blouse tucked into the waist of her stone washed blue jeans and a pair of high heel sandals. A simple strand of pearls was around her neck.

"Annie you look beautiful. You always look good in pearls. I feel a little underdressed in a polo and khakis."

"You look fine; just walk a couple steps behind me. Where are we going?"

"Remember that Italian restaurant Piacere that we always liked? It's been remodeled. Let's try it."

Right after Brett and Annie opened the office in 1984, a young guy named Bruno had come in without an appointment. He had a tooth that was killing him. Brett immediately diagnosed the crack in a molar, and when Bruno left with a temporary crown, the tooth felt great. As he walked out he handed Annie his card. He had just opened a new Italian restaurant six blocks away from the dental office. Brett and Annie tried it, loved it, and became regulars, eating there at least once a week. Since the divorce neither one of them had been back.

When Brett and Annie walked in, Bruno spotted them immediately. He came running up with a smile on his face. "Dr. Raven and Mrs..." He realized he didn't know by what name to call her.

Annie picked it up right away. "Just call me Annie, Bruno."

Bruno was truly excited. "I have a quiet table in the back. I used to save it just for you."

Brett ordered two glasses of the house red; however, when the waiter returned he had a bottle of champagne in his hand. "Bruno would like you to have this with his compliments."

Both Brett and Annie felt a little embarrassed but graciously accepted the wine. They tapped glasses together and sat in a reflective silence while sampling the bubbly drink.

The waiter returned and broke the silence. Annie said to Brett, "You order for both of us."

Brett asked the waiter to split the pear salad and ordered two plates of linguine with clams.

Halfway through the pasta, Brett asked Annie, "What exactly are you concerned about?"

Annie put down her fork and took a sip of wine. Well, first of all, I don't feel I deserve five million dollars. I'm not even sure I loved him."

Brett frowned. "That's not relevant; J.T. bought that policy because he felt you'd deserved it. If you don't want the money, give it to me. I'll buy a little jet to tool around in."

"Okay, okay, I get it. They're giving me the choice of a check or a wire transfer. What should I do?"

"You have your own bank account right?

Annie finished her glass of wine. "Sure, it has over two hundred thousand dollars in it."

Brett had to catch the noodles from dropping out of his open mouth. "Where the hell did you get two hundred thousand dollars?"

"From you actually. You've been giving me $4,000 a month for five years. I've been working at Nordstrom and other than clothes and jewelry, J.T. picked up all the bills."

Brett laughed. "Oh yeah, I forgot about that. Have them wire the money to that account. Once you get it we should make sure you spread it around a little; it's not good to have that much money in one bank. We'll have to find a new investment counselor, but I wouldn't worry about it right away. You're going to be a very popular woman at the banks."

"What about the house? The bank is pressuring me for the payments?"

Brett pushed the empty plate away from him. "Do you want to stay in it?"

"No, I told you before I don't even like the house."

"Then you have two choices. You can sell it for less than is owed on it, which means you'll have to pony up a half million dollars to the bank, or you can stay there another six months and just let the bank have it."

Annie looked shocked. "If I let the bank take it, won't it ruin my credit rating?"

Brett laughed out loud. "Annie, you have five million dollars. Who cares about your credit rating?"

Annie broke into a laugh also. "Yeah right! Who cares?"

They sat quietly for a few minutes savoring the last drops of the champagne.

Brett ordered two double decaf espressos and decided to change the conversation. "Did you know that guy who went down to Baja with J.T.?"

"No, J.T. told me he was a client from Minneapolis who loved fishing. Apparently the guy offered to pay for the fuel if J.T. would fly them down."

"Where did they stay?"

"Same place the three of us always stayed when we went fishing, Punta Pescadero."

Brett looked over the check and gave the waiter his American Express. "We'd better get going; it's a work day for us tomorrow."

Brett walked Annie to her door. The moment was awkward. Not knowing exactly what to do, Brett lifted his right arm to shake hands. Annie rose up on her tiptoes, put her hand on his shoulder, and gave him a peck on the cheek. "Thanks for dinner, I enjoyed it."

Two days later, Brett received a letter at his office from his aircraft insurance company.

Dear Mr. Raven:
General Aviation Insurance has completed its investigation into the accident of your insured aircraft, Beechcraft Baron 58, serial #C53422.
The preliminary NTSB report has determined that pilot error was the cause.
We have determined that John Thomas Talbot was current with his license and medical certificate at the time of the accident, therefore we will be sending you documents to sign and have notarized so that we may issue you a check for $190,000, the coverage on the hull minus the $10,000 deductible.
It is also our contractual obligation to inform you that the passenger's spouse filed a claim for wrongful death. We have agreed to issue an award of $1,250,000 to Maria Russo.
Sincerely,
Travis Rangle
Director of Claims

Brett did a little quick math: $5,000,000 to Annie, $4,250,000 to Maria Russo, $190,000 to him and another $1,250,000 to Maria. Brett concluded that March 12th, 2000 was a bad day for insurance companies.

Brett called the number on the letter from General Aviation Insurance and asked to speak with Mr. Rangle.

"Travis Rangle, what can I do for you?"

"Mr. Rangle, I just received a letter from you regarding the loss of my Baron 58."

"Was that the accident in Mexico?"

"Yes, that's it. I know that NTSB reports are

public information, I wondered if you could fax me a copy of their report."

Mr. Rangle paused for a moment obviously thinking about it. "I don't see why not; give me your fax number."

"By the way," Brett asked. "Why did the National Transportation Safety Board investigate an accident in Mexico?'

"It was a U.S. registry. Upon request from a U.S. insurance company they will do an investigation and issue a preliminary report. They don't guarantee there will be a final report."

Brett gave him the office fax, hung up, and went into the treatment room to place a filling. By the time he finished, Ginger had placed the fax on his desk.

Normally, when the NTSB investigates an airplane accident, they are extremely thorough. They note the weather to determine if it contributed to the accident. They examine what's left of the control surfaces and engines for possible failures which could have contributed to the accident. They also do toxicology tests on the blood and tissues of both the pilot and co-pilot. In the case of this accident, because the bodies were incinerated, those tests were not possible.

Brett examined the report. The beginning was the usual date, time, and place of the accident; the weather was noted as clear with visibility unrestricted. Toxicology was noted as unavailable. There was a lot of technical jargon which Brett skipped over and went straight to the findings involving the aircraft.

The airplane held 166 gallons of fuel. For some reason J.T. had re-filled his tanks after leaving Cabo San Lucas at a paved strip in Loreto, only two hundred miles north of Cabo. The Baron normally burned 16 gallons an hour out of each engine. The plane had been in flight for two hours since re-fueling, which meant the Baron had used 64 gallons, leaving 102 left in the tanks. The abundance of fuel was cited as the source of the explosion and fire. The board found no visible defects in the control surfaces that were salvaged. Examination of the instruments not destroyed indicated the auto pilot was locked in a nose down descent mode. The fact the pilot did not correct the setting before impact led them to the conclusion that he and his passenger had fallen asleep.

Brett put the report down on his desk. He didn't believe it. J.T. would never have put the autopilot into descent mode and then fallen asleep. The autopilot was an S-Tec 60-2 and Brett knew it by heart. It was quite sophisticated and had several settings available to the pilot. It could be programmed to hold the heading and the altitude enabling the plane to fly straight and level. It could also be set into the climb or descent mode allowing the pilot to choose the rate at which the plane would follow the command. If J.T. and his passenger were exhausted, he would have set the autopilot in the heading and altitude mode; falling asleep for an hour would not have been very wise, but it wouldn't have been fatal.

The only explanation for the autopilot being in the nose down descent mode without a correction by J.T. was a malfunction that couldn't have been corrected. Normally, there are three ways to disengage the autopilot: a push button switch on the control wheel, a toggle switch on the autopilot control panel and, if all fails, a circuit breaker on the electrical panel which can be pulled out.

Brett thought through a possible scenario. What if someone had changed the electronic input into the autopilot control panel so that the nose down mode, once selected, could not be disengaged? The disengage button on the control wheel could easily have been disabled by cutting its wires and the circuit breaker could have been bypassed by placing a simple wire shunt. J.T. would have been trying desperately to get the plane out of the descent, but it would have been impossible to do so.

Brett had a hunch. After lunch at the Sky Kitchen, he went across the airport to the only *fixed base operator* on the field, Peninsula Aviation, who maintained most of the planes based in San Carlos. He sought out the chief mechanic and struck up a conversation. "I'm thinking of buying a Cessna 206, are there any on the field?"

"Only one I know of, owned by a guy named Jennings."

Jackpot. "Do you guys take care of it?"

"I don't know if we do all his maintenance, but it's been in here several times."

"I'm curious. What model autopilot does he use for that type of airplane?"

The mechanic had to think for a minute. "Oh, I remember, our avionics department had to replace one of his servos. It's an S-Tec 60-2."

Chapter Eleven

Brett hadn't opened the doors to the hangar since J.T.'s death. He dialed in his combination, removed the padlock and slid the doors open. It was a lonely feeling. The Baron was destroyed and J.T. was dead. He really had no reason to be there, but he looked around and found everything was still neatly arranged as he had left it, except for the back right corner. The rear four seats of the Baron had been removed and were haphazardly shoved into the corner. Brett visualized the Baron without rear seats. There would have been an empty hold inside the double side doors, which could accommodate a huge amount of cargo—more space than J.T. would have needed for a fishing trip to Punta Pescadero.

Brett knew that he had to go down to Baja. There were too many strange circumstances surrounding both J.T.'s trip to Mexico and his fiery crash coming back.

Peninsula Aviation was only about two hundred yards from Brett's hangar. He entered through the double glass doors and was greeted by a cute little brunette about eighteen years old seated behind the reception desk. "Can I help you?"

Brett was peeking outside at the rental airplanes.

"Can I help you," the young lady said again.

Brett flashed back. "Oh, sorry, I was wondering if you have a plane I could rent for a trip to Baja."

"How long would you take it for?"

Brett did a little math calculation. It would take a day to get down, a day to get back, and it might take a couple days to gather some answers to the questions kicking around in his brain. "I'd probably need it for a week."

The brunette took out a folder and leafed through it. "The only aircraft we let go to Mexico is a Cessna 182RG. Are you qualified to fly it?"

"Yes, I have about twelve hundred hours and a thousand in complex retractable. What's the rate?"

The receptionist winced a bit. "It's expensive, a hundred and forty-five an hour plus fuel. It uses about fifteen gallons an hour, that will add about sixty more."

Brett wasn't surprised. "So, about two hundred an hour. How about insurance?"

"Peninsula has a policy; however, you'll have to pay the surcharge for coverage in Mexico, two hundred dollars for the week."

"Any other costs?"

"Most pilots also buy insurance from a Mexican company just in case there's a problem with Mexican authorities."

Brett remembered he and J.T. had used a company that bound coverage over the phone with a Mexican company. "I can take care of that myself; is it available next week?"

"It is. I'll have you fill out the application. You know you'll have to go up with the chief pilot for a check out?"

Brett figured he would, and mentally added another hundred dollars to the cost of the adventure. "Pencil me in to take it next Sunday. I'll do the check out this Friday on my day off."

When Brett got back to the office, he scribbled out the numbers for the trip. It was about thirteen hundred miles down and another thirteen hundred back. He could probably get 170 mph out of 182RG, which meant he would log over fifteen hours. At two hundred dollars an hour it would cost him about $3,000. Add the $200 cost of the American insurance, $200 more for Mexican insurance and $100 for the check out; he estimated $3,500 for the travel costs. Food and lodging would add another couple hundred, and he knew from experience there would be several hundred in additional costs. It was a lot of money, but he had to make this trip.

Brett gave Annie a call that evening. "How was your day off? I missed you today."

"Oh it was fine, I forgot how much time working takes. By the way, thanks for getting me out of the house."

"Hey, I got you cheap. I negotiated a great deal and the files look like they're almost finished."

Annie whispered, "Thanks again."

Brett wasn't going to tell Annie the suspicions he had about J.T.'s trip to Baja, but he had to let her know he was going down there. "I wanted to let you know I won't be at the office next week, I'm taking a trip down to Baja."

There was silence on the other end of the phone. Finally Annie spoke. "Brett, why?"

"I received the NTSB prelim report. It concluded that J.T. set the autopilot in a descent and then fell asleep. I can't accept that. I'm going to San Felipe and look at what's left of the Baron."

Annie sounded frightened. "Brett, it's so far to go by yourself in an airplane."

"Don't worry; San Felipe is less than a hundred miles from the border. I'll be back in a day or two." He lied.

"Promise me you'll be careful?"

"You know I will. I'll talk to you before I leave. Goodnight Annie."

Brett sat down and started to plan the flight. He laid out the charts and the airport guide on the kitchen table. He also took out a manual he had purchased several years ago which contained the airport information for Baja and a seven year old navigation chart for Mexico. He wasn't too concerned with its age; nothing changes very often in Mexico.

He decided to fly the route he had taken on

several previous flights to Baja. From San Carlos he would jump over to the San Joaquin Valley and head southeast passing over Bakersfield and Palm Springs until he reached the Mexican border near Calexico.

Baja is a peninsula, which extends seven hundred and fifty miles south from its border with California. It's separated from mainland Mexico on the east by the Gulf of California, and on the west and south coastline it meets the Pacific Ocean.

After crossing the border, navigation would be simple; fly along the gulf and keep water on the left and land on the right.

Brett planned his stops. After crossing the border he would have to land in Mexicali, a port of entry into Mexico. From Mexicali he would fly a hundred miles south to San Felipe, the town thirty miles north of the accident. Although he told Annie this was his final destination, his actual plan was to continue south for six hundred fifty miles, with stops in Loreto, Punta Pescadero and Cabo San Lucas.

After the flight planning, he placed the charts, manuals and plans into his leather shoulder bag.

Chapter Twelve

On Friday Brett stopped at Peninsula Aviation, flew his check ride with the chief pilot, signed the papers, and picked up the keys to the Cessna 182RG. Saturday he pulled a small duffle off the top shelf of the closet and threw in a few basics: shaving kit, underwear, a pair of jeans, a pair of shorts, a couple polo shirts, some socks, an extra pair of sneakers, and a sweat shirt.

He packed his leather shoulder bag, went into his office, and removed a close up photo of himself posing with J.T. next to the Baron. He also selected two close ups he had taken from his car of Claude Jennings. He tossed in his wallet, his passport, and finally an envelope in which he had put ten, one hundred dollars bills and twenty-five, twenty dollar bills.

Brett called Annie Saturday night. "Hi, Annie, just wanted to remind you I'm leaving for Baja tomorrow."

"I know, why am I worried?"

"You shouldn't be, I've done this a dozen times, I'll be fine. By the way, if the fishing is good out of San Felipe, I'm going to take a couple days of R&R, so I might not get home till Wednesday or Thursday."

"Be careful Brett. I don't know what I'd do if I lost two friends to Mexico."

"I'll see you by the end of the week."

The alarm was set for six a.m. Brett was awake at five just staring at the clock. He got out of bed at five-thirty, showered, didn't shave, and threw on his clothes for the trip. He felt an anxious excitement, which took away his appetite, but he managed to force down a bowl of cereal and milk. He skipped the coffee, not wanting to have the urge to later use the 'porta-potty'. On his way out of the house he grabbed a half dozen bottles of water from the garage and tossed them on the back seat with his bags.

Since Brett had only flown this plane for forty-five minutes, while getting checked out for the rental, he took a good half hour doing his pre-flight inspection. Everything looked good and by seven-thirty he broke ground from the runway heading south. He leveled off at seventy-five hundred feet, adjusted the power setting for cruise speed and called the Flight Service Station to open his VFR flight plan.

"Oakland radio, this is Cessna four five four

five Tango."

"Four five four five Tango, this is Oakland Flight Service, go ahead."

"Four five Tango would like to open its VFR flight plan from San Carlos to Mexicali, Mexico. We were off San Carlos at seven thirty-six."

"Four five Tango your flight plan is open. What is your estimated time for border crossing?"

"Four five Tango estimates border crossing at ten-thirty local time."

"Copy that. Give San Diego radio a call to update your crossing time about ten minutes before the border. Have a good flight."

"See ya. Four five Tango."

The weather was clear and Brett had a decent tail wind which increased his ground speed by about twelve mph. When his distance measuring instrument read fifteen minutes to Mexicali, he dialed up 122.4 on his number two radio. "San Diego Flight Service, Cessna four five four five Tango on 122.4"

"Four five Tango, San Diego radio. Go ahead."

"Four five Tango is on a VFR flight plan from San Carlos, California to Mexicali. My estimated time for border crossing is ten-twenty local."

"Okay, I've got it. No need to close your flight plan, we'll do it. Good flight."

"Thanks, four five Tango."

Mexicali airport is located about a mile from the border. Brett dialed in 118.2, the tower frequency on his number one radio. Every control tower in the world that handles international air traffic uses English as its universal language, and Brett made his radio call with ease. "Mexicali tower, Cessna four five four five Tango five miles from border crossing, landing Mexicali."

The controller answered with a slight accent to his English. "Good morning, four five Tango, enter left downwind for runway two eight, report downwind."

Brett entered the traffic pattern, reported as directed, and landed on runway two eight. He took a left turn off the runway and taxied to the customs office.

Brett had been through this drill before. Mexican customs is quite different from it's counterpart in the United States. Rarely is the airplane or the luggage inspected. The entire process of going through customs, registering your airplane and filing a Mexican flight plan, is designed to create employment for as many people as possible without really accomplishing any worthwhile tasks.

A man in an olive green uniform wearing a gold badge greeted Brett as he exited the Cessna with his leather shoulder bag. "Buenos Dias, Señor."

"Buenos Dias." Brett replied. "Should I go into the office?"

"Uno momento." The agent replied as he started to look seriously at Brett's plane.

Brett reached into his bag and pulled out a

twenty dollar bill. He handed it to the agent and said, "Muchas gracias."

The serious look changed to a smile as the officer took the twenty. "De nada, you may go into the office."

Inside the office there were two desks occupied by non-uniformed civilians dressed in jeans and work shirts. Brett walked up to the first desk and gave him his passport. The man produced the same serious look as had been displayed by the agent outside. Brett spotted the open drawer with several US bills in it, took another twenty from his bag and dropped it in the drawer. The clerk acknowledged the donation with a head nod, stamped an official looking piece of paper in three different places, and pointed to the next desk.

The man at this desk spoke excellent English. He asked from where Brett had departed, where he was going in Baja, and a few other innocuous questions. Brett dropped a twenty dollar bill into his drawer. "Thank you sir, if there's anything else you need, please let me know. If you will step into the next office, you will be able to file a flight plan for Mexico."

Brett noted his name tag. "Thanks, Juan."

Brett walked into the adjoining office and sat down at the desk. The clerk spoke reasonable English and asked where Brett was going and how long he would be in Baja. He put two sheets of paper separated by a carbon into an old black typewriter with Underwood emblazed in gold letters. He slowly prepared a Mexican flight plan. Brett didn't pay much attention, because he knew the flight plan was just a formality and it would be filed and never looked at again. The clerk handed Brett the carbon copy. Brett dropped a twenty into the open drawer. "Gracias," he said as he left the desk.

Brett went back into the first room where no one was working; he was the only pilot who had checked in that morning. He spotted the English speaking clerk. "Juan, there is something you could help me with."

"Certainly, Señor Raven, what can I do for you?"

The crash was on March 12th. J.T. had left San Carlos five days earlier on March 7th. Brett picked up a pencil and paper from Juan's desk. He wrote down March 7, 2000. Under the date he wrote N123GS, the number of the Baron 58, and N206CJ, the number of Claude's Cessna 206. He placed a one hundred dollar bill on top of the paper and handed it to Juan. "Could you look up the flight plans for this date? I'd like to know if these two airplanes filed plans and to where they were filed."

Juan was delighted. "Certainly, it will only take a couple minutes. Please sit down."

Juan returned with two flight plans which obviously had been typed on the old Underwood. Both pilots had checked through Mexicali on March 7th. The Baron listed Punta

Pescadero as its destination and the 206 listed San Jose Del Cabo, the airport servicing Cabo San Lucas, as its next stop.

"Thanks Juan, I'll see you in a few days on my way back home."

Juan flashed a big smile. "My pleasure, Señor Raven, my pleasure."

Brett topped off the fuel tanks and took off for San Felipe, only forty minutes away. Other than three or four large airports in Baja, none, including San Felipe, had control towers. He announced his arrival on the common traffic advisory frequency for anyone who might be listening, landed on the five thousand foot strip, and taxied to an empty cinderblock shack with graffiti sprayed all over it.

He tied the airplane down with a couple ropes anchored to the pavement, took out his two cases and locked the airplane. There was no one around; however, Brett suspected there was only one cab in town and the driver would have spotted his incoming plane as future business. As predicted, five minutes later an old four door 1979 Chevy Impala with the word Taxi hand painted on its door drove up.

"Taxi, Señor?"

Brett grabbed his bags and tossed them onto the back seat. "Si, Gracias." He had looked up the three hotels in town. "Econohotel, por favor."

"Si, Si." The driver said, raising a cloud of dust

from the pavement as he drove off.

The hotel probably looked new in nineteen-fifty, but in the year two thousand it looked a hundred years old. Brett registered, went to his room and checked for bed bugs and running water. He went down to the lobby and addressed the English speaking desk clerk. "Did you hear about the plane crash just south of here last March?"

"Si, Señor Raven, it has been a tourist attraction for the pilots who fly in."

Brett wasn't surprised and handed a twenty to the clerk. "Could you arrange a driver to take me there?"

"No problem, I'll have a driver here in twenty minutes."

Brett was in the bar drinking a Corona from the bottle when the desk clerk caught his eye and pointed toward the entrance. Brett took one last slug on the beer and headed for the door.

It was only thirty miles, but the driver couldn't get more than forty miles an hour out of the Chevy, making the trip almost an hour long. The driver turned off the main road onto a dirt one and continued on for about a mile. He stopped the car and pointed to a dark pile three hundred yards from the road. Brett got out, motioned the driver to wait, and headed to the wreck.

When he reached the wreckage, he had to subdue a wave of nausea. The beautiful blue and brown Baron, which used to be his pride and joy, was charred black. The nose of the plane looked like an accordion, squeezed in the closed position. The right engine was off the plane and the left one was still attached and the color of charcoal. Both wings had explosion scars, where the hundred and two gallons of gas had ignited. One of the double side doors was still in place, but the one near the rear was missing.

Brett walked to the right side of the plane, where the door was missing and peeked inside. The back seats were gone, which was no surprise, since he had seen them in the corner of his hangar a couple days ago. In their place was a pile of ash, where apparently the cargo had burned to cinders. He tested the integrity of the burned out airplane floor and crawled inside to get a view of the cockpit. The front seats were burned down to the wire springs and he squeezed through them to inspect the instruments; he wanted to look at the autopilot. To his surprise, all of the instruments were gone. Apparently the locals had pirated them either as souvenirs or as items to sell. He went back to the car and motioned the driver back to town. As the car drove off, he didn't bother to look back.

Brett awoke early on Monday morning, managed to get a trickle of water for a shower and dressed. He didn't shave. He paid the twenty-eight dollars for the room, paid a dollar for an apple and arranged for the town taxi to take him to the airport.

The trip to Loreto was a little over five hundred

miles and it took Brett three hours. Loreto is one of those few airports which services commercial air traffic in Baja; therefore, it has a long runway and a control tower. Brett was given instructions to land to the north; he circled out over the water of the gulf and entered his final approach to runway three four.

As he taxied up to the gas pumps, a large guy in a uniform carrying a rifle on a sling over his shoulder approached. Brett was used to this charade and he took a twenty out of his envelope. After exiting the plane, Brett cordially said, "Buenos dias. Como esta?"

"Muy bien, gracias. Identification please."

Brett handed him his passport with the currency inside.

The guard put the bill in his pocket and handed the passport back to Brett. He put the passport back in his bag and said, "Señor, you speak English, correct."

"Yes."

Brett took out one of his hundred dollar bills. The soldier spotted it. "Are you the only guard for this airport?"

The soldier kept his eye on the bill. "Si, yes, I am."

Brett took the picture of him with J.T. in front of the Baron out of his pack. "Do you remember this man or this airplane? It was in here last March."

The guard put down his rifle and took the

picture. He concentrated fully. He wanted the hundred. Finally he said, "Yes, I do."

"What makes you think you remember?"

"It was a beautiful plane, two engines. The pilot tipped me twenty dollars."

Brett was skeptical. "Anything else you remember?"

"Yes, when he took off, one of the side doors was open. It was knocking against the side of the plane."

Brett stuffed the hundred into the shirt pocket of the guard. "Muchas gracias, Señor. Thanks a lot."

As Brett taxied out for takeoff, the guard was smiling and waving.

The trip to Punta Pescadero took exactly an hour. There was no control tower; however, there was no air traffic either. Brett buzzed the hotel to let them know he was landing and circled to land to the east on runway one one. By the time he had the plane tied down, an old WWII jeep arrived to take him to the lobby.

"Have room for me tonight?" Brett inquired.

The desk clerk was an American. "You kidding? We don't get many tourists in the summer, too hot. Where you coming in from?"

"California, I'll only be one night, I'm headed down to Cabo tomorrow." He put his passport and credit card on the desk.

"Ever been here before?"

Brett developed a nostalgic smile. "Yes, my

wife and I used to come here often."

"Well, welcome back. You know meals are included. You'll have time for a shower before dinner."

Brett signed for the room and slipped his credit card back into his wallet. "I was wondering if you could do me a favor."

The clerk smiled. "I will, if I can."

"I met a guy who was down here last March. He said the fishing was great, but he couldn't remember the exact dates he was here. Could you look it up for me?"

The clerk took out a register and flipped back three months. "What's his name?"

"Talbot, John T. Talbot."

The American ran his finger down the register. "Here it is. He was here on March 7th, but I don't think he did much fishing, he checked out on the 8th."

"I knew I shouldn't get fishing tips from a guy in a bar, thanks anyway. By the way, did he have a buddy with him?"

"Maybe, we only list the person who pays the bill."

Brett was in no hurry on Tuesday morning. San Jose del Cabo was only sixty miles south, twenty minutes by plane. He had breakfast on the terrace overlooking the pool and the deep blue water of the gulf. His mind wandered as he sipped his coffee. What great times the three us of had here. We sat at this exact table every morning and planned our adventures for the day. Before he could sink deep into melancholy, the waitress placed a huge helping of huevos rancheros along with a basket of warm tortillas on the table.

An hour later Brett felt a pang of anxiety as he pointed the Cessna toward the tip of the Baja Peninsula. Tomorrow would be the day he hoped to find the reason J.T. had come to Mexico last March.

As Brett swung the Cessna over the southern tip of Cabo San Lucas in preparation for landing, he was struck again, as he had been several times before, by the contrast in living conditions he observed beneath him. Built on the hillsides were million dollar condominiums and in the marina were parked multi-million dollar yachts. On the edges of town, people were living in cardboard shacks.

San Jose del Cabo, the airport servicing the resort town, is located about fifteen miles north and is the largest airport on the peninsula. Everyday commercial and private jets land to drop off tourists. As Brett taxied into the parking area, it wasn't difficult to tell, that his plane was the smallest on the ramp.

Cabo is different from the other airports in Baja. There is a large terminal building with sharply dressed employees scurrying around. Inside the building a beautiful waiting area contains luxurious furnishings and numerous amenities. A car rental agency has a spot in the corner, and there is a lounge nearby, where pilots can relax or do their flight planning.

Brett registered the Cessna at the front desk and arranged for a rental car. While the attendant was fetching the car, Brett stepped out of the terminal and headed for the gas pumps. He had already arranged for a fill up; however, he wanted to talk to the attendants. Most of the planes on the ramp were usually of U.S. registry, so the captain of the fueling area was fluent in English.

Brett knew the information would cost more here, so he took two, hundred dollar bills, from his cache. He also took out the pictures of J.T and Claude. "Excusa Señor, habla Ingles?"

"Yes. What can I do for you?"

Brett flashed the bills. "I was hoping you or one of your guys could help me with some information."

The captain was not going to let two hundred dollars slip away. "Anything you want."

"These two men were here three months ago. I'd like to know, if anyone noticed what was being loaded into their planes."

The manager took the pictures, but Brett held onto the two hundred. "I don't need to ask anyone, I can give you the information you're looking for."

Brett waited, but there was only silence. He took a chance and slipped the two bills into the captain's hand.

The man stuffed the bills into his pants pocket. "The short fat guy comes in here about every three months. The good looking guy I only saw once back in March. Both of them took care of me real good."

Brett had to milk all the information out that he could. "Why do you think the fat guy comes here every three months?"

"He picks up cargo and takes it back to the states."

"What kind of cargo?"

The informant just scratched his head. Brett took out another hundred dollar bill and said. "This is it, take it but don't play any more games with me."

The captain snatched the bill. "A government van always pulls up to his airplane escorted by a police car. The guys in the van usually load two large crates into the back of his plane."

"What's in the crates?"

"I have no clue other than I know they must be freezing cold."

Brett frowned. "Why would you think that?"

"The guys loading them always wear thermal insulating gloves."

Brett changed the subject. "What about the good looking guy? Was he in the same plane with the fat guy?"

The captain looked a little perplexed. "No, he was in the same plane you showed me in the picture. Big twin engine job."

"Did he have the same cargo?"

"It looked the same, two large crates."

"Did you get a look at that guy's passenger?"

"I didn't get real close. The police uniforms keep us at a distance."

Brett was pretty sure he had extracted all the information that three hundred dollars would buy; however, he tried one more question. "Back in March, do you remember what time the two guys took off?"

The captain looked a little pissed off that no more money was coming his way. "I remember the fat guy took off a couple hours before the big twin." He waited, hoping for another bill, and then began to walk away. "Hey, buddy, I gotta go. Thanks for the gratuity."

Brett picked up his Ford Taurus in front of the terminal, threw his bags in the back seat, and turned onto the road leading to Cabo San Lucas.

Brett's favorite hotel in Cabo was the Finisterra. He loved driving the narrow winding road to the top of the rocky peak where it was located; it gave him an unobstructed view of the Marina, the Gulf, and the famous natural stone archway, Los Arcos.

He checked in at the front desk and negotiated a premium room for only forty dollars. The temperature was ninety-eight degrees and very few tourists were looking for accommodations.

Brett showered, decided to shave and take a two hour nap. He put on a pair of shorts and a polo shirt and walked the three blocks to the downtown area. He knew where he was headed. The usual hangout for the Three Musketeers had always been Carlos'n'Charlie's, a bar-restaurant on the main drag.

Because of the lack of tourists, the oak bar with the brass railing was occupied mainly by locals. Brett sat down and ordered a Pacifico along with a plate of chicken-potato enchiladas with tomatillo sauce. He had forgotten how tasty real Mexican food was.

As he was mopping up the sauce with a piece of tortilla, a young fellow pulled up the stool next to him. "You are an American, si?"

Brett sized him up. He was obviously a local, but he spoke pretty descent English. "Yes I am, name's Brett."

"I'm Carlos, like the restaurant, nice to meet you." Brett took a liking to the guy right away. "Where did you learn your English?"

"Right here actually. There are always Americans at the bar, that's why I come in. They teach me good English."

Brett laughed, this was an unlikely classroom. He bought Carlos a beer and they chatted for about an hour. It was getting late and Brett had to get some sleep; however, before he left he asked Carlos, "Where are the government offices for Los Cabos?"

"Which ones are you looking for?"

"Well it may sound strange, but I want to talk

to the Coroner or the Medical Examiner."

Carlos did not inquire why. "You're very lucky, Dr. Rivera is both."

"How would I locate him?"

Carlos asked the bartender for a pencil and proceeded to draw a map on a cocktail napkin. "You can't get lost; it's only a mile out of town."

They shook hands and Brett went back to the Finisterra to get some sleep.

Wednesday's weather looked like a carbon copy of Tuesday's. The forecast was for ninety-nine degrees. After finishing breakfast, Brett located the Taurus, tossed the cocktail napkin on the passenger seat and headed out of town. Carlos's directions were perfect. Brett pulled up in front of a slump stone structure displaying a placard that read, El Medico Forense de Los Cabos.

The inside of the building had a strange smell: a combination of rice, beans and formaldehyde. Brett approached a young girl who was busily filing her nails; he took out his dental business card, and handed it to her. "Como esta, Doctor Rivera por favor."

The secretary sensing that her English may be better than Brett's Spanish replied. "He is in the dissection room. You can wait a half hour maybe?"

"No problem." He took a seat on a rusted card table chair.

An hour later a good looking man in a white jacket appeared in the doorway of the adjoining room. Brett recognized him immediately from the photograph in Claude's office. "Doctor Raven, I'm Doctor Rivera, what can I do for you?" He spoke English without a trace of an accent.

"Could I have a few minutes of your time?"

"Certainly, come into my office."

The office was covered with posters of human anatomy. There was a skeleton in the corner and a skull on the desk. Dr. Rivera motioned Brett to take a seat across from his desk. "So what brings an American dentist to the office of a Mexican Pathologist?"

Brett leaned back and tried not to look nervous. "I'm down here on a fishing trip and I ran into a doctor who told me about your experiments with cryonics. He said you were an expert and probably one of the world's leaders in the field."

Dr. Rivera smiled. "That's very flattering; however, there are many doctors doing experiments in the field. I'm curious, how does cryonics relate to dentistry?"

"I'm not sure, that's why I wanted to talk to you. I've volunteered time doing forensic dentistry and I'm acquainted with the recently deceased. I've always wondered if the bones of mastication, the maxilla and mandible, could be preserved for future use."

Dr. Rivera appeared to be interested. "I've never tried to preserve bone. "I work mainly with vital organs such as kidneys, hearts, livers."

"Have you been successful in maintaining those tissues adequately to be used in future transplants?"

Miguel Rivera put his two index fingers together as if preparing to give a lecture. "My research has proven that by immediately lowering the temperature of organs from a deceased, down to two hundred degrees below zero, it is possible to maintain them for transplantation up to several years in the future."

Brett was actually getting interested. "How do you get temperatures down that low?"

"It's quite simple. We use machinery which employs the use of liquid nitrogen."

"Incredible! Why aren't doctors following cryonic procedures?"

"That's the problem with medicine today. Hundreds of thousand of lives could be saved, but until research has been done for ten or twenty years, doctors won't use these organs. They only transplant the ones which have been recently harvested."

Brett was getting to the point of his visit. "What if a doctor, say in the U.S., wanted to use a cryonic preserved organ? How would you get it there without it thawing out and becoming useless?"

Miguel was enjoying his lecture. "It's not that complicated. Once the tissues are frozen to two hundred below zero, they can be packed in between massive amounts of dry ice. They will maintain temperature for two to four days before being placed back into a liquid nitrogen machine."

Brett feigned amazement. "How big a crate

would you need to pack a heart, if it was being transported for future transplantation?"

"Well, that is a slight problem. The organ would have to be surrounded by four feet of dry ice."

"You mean the crate would be four feet long and four feet high?"

"Exactly, however, if two organs were to be transported at once, it could be done with one crate six feet long and four feet high, because they would share the ice which is packed between them."

Brett wanted to get one more question in. "Have you ever tested this transport system?"

Dr. Rivera anticipated that question. "We've tested the system, but obviously we have never actually transported any cryonic organs because there is no market anywhere to use them."

Brett got up to leave. "Well, I thank very much for the information, Dr. Rivera. I don't know, if your process has any application to dentistry, however I'm going to think on it."

Dr. Rivera pushed his chair back and shook Brett's hand. "It was my pleasure."

Brett drove back to the hotel to retrieve his bags and check out. If he took off by noon he might be able to get home by ten o'clock that evening. He loaded the car and headed for the airport,

About five miles north of town Brett caught sight of a flashing blue and red light in his rear view mirror and he pulled over. The police car pulled up behind him and two uniformed officers got out and came to the driver side window. Brett rolled it down. "I'm an American, just on my way back to the airport, anything wrong?"

"Pasaporte." The officer said gruffly.

Brett didn't like the situation. It wasn't uncommon for tourists to be shaken down for a bribe by the police. He reached into his bag and removed his passport along with a hundred dollar bill, which he placed inside it.

The policeman opened the passport, took out the bill and placed it in his shirt pocket. "Fuera, out."

Brett got out of the car. He felt a bolt of lightning above his left eye, where the ring on the cop's right index finger split the skin above his eyebrow. He went down on one knee. The uniform kicked him in the stomach. All the air went out of his lungs and he started gasping for breath.

The pugnacious officer pulled him to his feet and cuffed him. Brett could taste the blood that was dripping from his eyebrow down onto his upper lip as he tried to fill his lungs with oxygen. The cop shoved him in the back seat of the patrol car and drove off with the other officer following in Brett's rental car.

They took him back to town and pulled up in front of a decrepit building which housed the police station. No one spoke as Brett was taken inside, led down to the end of dark hall and into a barred cell. The tough cop took off the handcuffs and pushed Brett inside.

The cell was very dark; however, Brett could make out a cot and an open hole in the floor, which was apparently his toilet. There was no air conditioning and the temperature was at least ten degrees hotter than outside. The smell was foul: a combination of urine, feces and vomit. In the corner there was a basin with a water faucet, but Brett was afraid to drink out of it for fear of getting sick. No one looked in on him and after the sun went down it was completely dark in the cell. He laid down on the cot; sleep was impossible.

At nine the next morning a guard opened the cell and motioned Brett to follow him. They went down the dark hall to an office where the guard poked Brett in the back signaling him to enter. Brett opened the door and there stood the other man in Claude's photo, Police Chief Jorge Rivera. "Sit down, Dr. Raven. Interesting eye shadow you have on."

Brett complied.

"I understand you are interested in cryonics."

"Yes, is that a crime in Mexico?"

Jorge lit an unfiltered cigarette. "It really doesn't matter if it's a crime or not. I decide who goes to jail and how long they stay. How did you like the accommodations?"

"Not quite up to the Ritz Carlton."

Chief Rivera gave a wry smile and inhaled a drag from his cigarette. As he exhaled, he said, "I heard you were a smart ass. Here's the deal Raven. Your car is out front. You're going to get in it and drive to the airport. Then, you'll get in that Cessna and fly as fast as you can back to California. If I ever see you in Baja again, that cell will be your personal Ritz Carlton. Do you get it?"

"I get it."

"Good, and as they say in your country, have a nice day."

As Brett opened the door to leave, Rivera spoke again. "Be careful flying home. I'd hate to see you wind up like your friend Mr. Talbot."

Brett turned the car in at the airport and took his bags into the pilot lounge. He looked at himself in the mirror. He was a mess. He had a deep vertical cut above his left eyebrow which was covered with dried blood stuck to the hair. His eye was purple and slightly shut. The white polo shirt he wore was stained red across the front and the underarms were brown from sweat.

He threw the shirt in the waste basket and put on a clean one from his bag. He washed the blood from his face, but couldn't hide the technicolor eye. As he brushed his hair, he looked again in the mirror and mouthed to himself, "Are you stupid or just plain nuts?"

He filed the obligatory flight plan and dropped a twenty in the drawer. He had the paranoid notion that perhaps his plane had been sabotaged as J.T.'s had, so he spent a half hour checking every system and instrument. When he was convinced all was well, he strapped on his lap belt and shoulder harness for the trip home.

It took Brett five and half hours to reach Mexicali. Checking out of Mexico was easier than checking in; there was only one desk to stop at. "Señor Raven, did you have a nice stay in Baja? Oh my God, what happened to your eye?" It was Juan.

"Oh, hello Juan. Yes, it was lovely, really lovely. I slipped on the deck of the fishing boat."

Juan gave a compassionate smile and filled out Brett's departure papers.

The regulations to re-enter the United States required Brett to give a thirty minute notice before crossing the border. He did so and landed at Calexico, California, just five miles from Mexicali. A U.S. customs agent inspected his plane and gave him a document approving his entry. Brett decided to ask a question. "Believe me, I'm not planning to smuggle anything in, but I'm curious, how do you guys know I just flew in from Mexico? Couldn't a smuggler cross the border and drop stuff off at a nearby airport, give you a thirty minute notice and then show up?"

The agent looked at him with squinted eyes. "They probably could, but, if we catch them, they're looking at ten to twenty in a federal prison." Then the agent smiled. "You're not looking to smuggle in a dental drill, are you doc? You look pretty sinister with that shiner." They both laughed and Brett jumped into his plane for the last leg home.

Chapter Thirteen

Brett touched down in San Carlos just before midnight. By the time he secured the plane, picked up his car and drove up the hill to his townhouse, it was one o'clock Friday morning. He was exhausted, but he couldn't get into bed without washing the Mexican jail off his skin. He let the hot water massage his body for twenty minutes before getting out of the shower and throwing on a robe. He picked up the pile of dirty clothes, threw them into the washer, turned the water temperature to hot, and pushed the start button. Back in his room he collapsed stark naked into bed and slept for twelve hours.

Most of the staff was off on Friday; however, Ginger was in the office to answer phones and make appointments. Brett walked in through the business office. Ginger looked up. "Well, well, if it's not Charles Lindbergh. How was the flight to Mexico?"

"Relaxing, very relaxing." Brett replied as he picked up a twelve inch pile of mail which had been saved for him.

"My God, what happened to your eye?"

"I walked into the wall trying to find the bathroom."

Ginger giggled. "I don't buy that one. Are you going to see some patients next week? The natives are getting restless."

Brett laughed. "Yeah, yeah, I'll work through some lunches next week to catch up. Go ahead and fill in the times."

"Annie has been worried sick about you. She said you were expected home by Wednesday."

Brett frowned. "I'll give her a call as soon as I work through this mail." He went back to his private office.

He went through the motions of opening mail, but his mind was churning a hundred miles an hour. Who the hell was Tony Russo? Why did he return to the U.S.? Why had he contacted J.T.? What was he doing on that trip? Brett knew he had to find the answers.

He threw the junk mail in the waste basket and picked up the phone. Annie answered on the first ring. "Hey, Annie, it's me."

"Are you home?"

"Safe and sound."

Annie sighed. "I was worried; I expected you home by Wednesday night."

"Sorry, I stayed a couple extra days."

"I didn't mean to sound like your mother. I'm sure you don't need that right now."

Brett felt a little guilty for deceiving her. "Annie, I like the idea of someone worrying about me. I apologize for not contacting you; can I make it up to you? How about dinner tonight?"

"Where you taking me?"

"How about ribs at McArthur Park? I'll pick you up at seven-thirty."

Brett parked his Porsche in the driveway and knocked twice on the door. Annie yelled, "Come on in."

Brett sat down on the family room couch. His mind was still wandering. Who the hell was Tony Russo?

Annie appeared. "Hi."

Brett turned around. Annie went pale. "Wow, what happened to your eye?"

"I took a header getting out of the plane in San Felipe."

"Did you get it stitched?"

"Na, I'll like a scar, make me look macho. Let's go."

McArthur Park was in Palo Alto and was well known for its slow cooked spare ribs. Annie ordered a small rack and Brett opted for the full one. Annie said, "How 'bout a beer with the ribs."

"As long as its not Mexican beer. I've had enough of Mexico for awhile."

They settled into their ribs before Annie finally broached the subject. "How was Baja? I get the feeling you were disappointed."

Brett put down a rib and took a gulp from his Coors Lite. "The plane was burnt to a crisp and the autopilot was stolen."

"Oh, I'm sorry. I know you feel an obligation to get J.T. off the hook."

"Yeah, well, I guess that's not going to happen."

Annie's mood changed. "Brett, let it go, its going to eat you up inside if you don't."

"The last words J.T. said to me were 'you don't owe me', but I still feel that I do."

"You mean for saving your retirement fund?"

"Yeah, he didn't have to do that. He could have let me go down the tubes." Brett pushed some French fries around his plate with his fork. "I've tried to disengage, but I can't seem to let go."

"Promise me you'll try harder."

"Okay, I Promise." He lied again.

Their walk to the door was not as strained as the last time. Brett gave Annie a peck on the cheek and said goodnight.

Brett couldn't get to sleep. He was obsessed with the need to find out the mystery of Tony Russo. He decided he would track down Tony's wife Maria, and then he nodded off.

Chapter Fourteen

Monday was a hectic day at the office. Luckily the ten o'clock patient cancelled at the last minute and Brett was able to grab a cup of coffee and take a break in his private office. He opened his top drawer and rummaged through it for Claude Jennings phone number.

Brett dialed the number. "Jennings."

"Mr. Jennings, this is Brett Raven, J.T.'s friend."

After a couple moments of silence, Claude responded. "The fuck you want?"

"I've come upon some information I think you would be interested in hearing."

Jennings was angry. "I don't want to hear anything you have to say and I'm getting tired of you sticking your nose in my business."

"Come on Claude, wouldn't you rather hear it from me than the FBI?

The phone was silent again. "Okay, but if I

don't like where the conversation is going, I'm not going to kick your ass out of the office like last time, I'm just plain going to kick your ass."

Brett wasn't too concerned. "I get it Claude, when can we talk?"

"Be here at two."

Brett had a couple patients at two so he asked Ginger to reschedule them. He promised to be back by three.

The door was ajar, Brett walked in. Claude was behind his desk puffing on a foul smelling cigar. "Sit down, asshole."

Brett took a seat in the same chair he had sat in the last time. "I just returned from Baja."

"Yeah, I heard you were down there. Guess you spent a day in the slammer. How did you like it?"

"I see you've been in contact with the Rivera brothers."

Jennings ignored the remark. "So what information do you have for me?"

Brett pulled his chair closer to the desk. "I found out you flew to Baja on the same day as J.T. and you flew back the day he was killed. The accident report blamed J.T. for misuse of his 60-2 autopilot. I know that your Cessna 206 has an S-Tec 60-2."

Claude's face flushed red. "Whoa, hold it right there. Are you implying that I sabotaged his airplane?"

"Did you?"

"Why would I?"

"J.T. horned in on your deal in Mexico and was cutting into your action. You were going to lose money and, if J.T got caught, he might spill what he knew about you to the authorities. I know you threatened him."

The angry red faced turned pale and a glimpse of fear appeared. "Look, first of all, I didn't kill J.T. He found out about my dealings in Baja and pretty much blackmailed me into helping him make a deal. I went down there to meet my contacts and make sure his deal went smoothly. If I wanted to kill him, I would have strangled the bastard."

"Tell me about his deal."

"No can do. That would be incriminating myself. I'm taking the fifth."

Brett decided he would try a bluff. "What happens if I go to the FBI?"

"You won't do that."

"What makes you think so?"

Claude called his bluff. "We both know if you do, your buddy's name is going to be smeared all over the newspapers and TV stations. You'd also have to watch your back for friends of the Rivera brothers."

Brett was on the defensive now. "Okay Claude, no FBI, but, if I learn you were involved in J.T.'s death, all bets are off."

"I'm good with that."

Brett got up to leave. "One more thing, did you know the guy who was with J.T., Tony Russo?"

"I never met him before the trip to Mexico."

Brett opened the door and quoted Claude from their last meeting. "Stay in touch." He slammed it behind him.

Chapter Fifteen

Brett was awake all night thinking about Tony Russo. He was the missing link; he could feel it in his bones. Who was he? Why did he come back from Italy? Why did he go to Mexico with J.T.?

It was seven-thirty on Saturday morning, the coffee maker had started grinding beans, and Brett was still lying awake. He dragged himself out of bed, splashed cold water on his face and walked downstairs. The *Chronicle* always arrived before seven so he turned off the alarm, opened the front door, and scooped up the newspaper.

The paper was filled with the usual: rising prices, rising crime, and rising temperatures. He sipped his coffee and leafed through the pages.

Tucked into a filler space on page fourteen was a two inch article that froze him.

Airplane Crash In Mexico Blamed On Pilot Error

The National Transportation Board has determined that the crash of a Beechcraft twin engine plane, killing the pilot and a passenger, near San Felipe, Mexico on March 12, 2000 was the result of the pilot's misuse of his autopilot. The case has been closed.

Brett mumbled to himself. "Oh J.T., what did you do? What did you get yourself into? Goddamn it, I'm gonna find out."

His briefcase was on the coffee table in the living room. He sifted through it until he came upon the notes he had made at J.T.'s office on which he had written Tony's Minneapolis address.

Upstairs he powered up his iMac. On the internet he found a site that would match an address to a phone number. He looked at his notes and typed in 2651 Golden Valley Terrace, Minneapolis, Minnesota. Up jumped the number: 612-958-2376.

Brett dialed the number and a female voice answered. "Hello."

"Hello, is this Maria Russo?"

There was a short silence. "Oh, I think you're looking for the previous owner. We bought the house from her a month ago, and we just moved in last Monday."

Brett felt crushed. He had missed her by less than a week. "Did she leave a forwarding address? I'm an old friend of her husband's and I have to get in touch with her."

"I'm really sorry. She told us about the plane accident. I guess she just couldn't stand to stay in the house without him. She didn't actually leave any forwarding address."

Brett wasn't going to give up. "Did she mention anything that would indicate where she might have moved?"

The woman thought for a moment. "Now that you mention it, she said she was going back to Italy, where her husband's family lives. She said it was a small town near Florence."

"Did she leave anything behind in the house?"

The woman laughed. "If she did, we won't find it for a month. We've got boxes everywhere."

The conversation was exhausted. "Would you take my number? If you find anything of Maria's, I'd like to know about it. I going to try and find her and if I do, perhaps I could get the belongings to her."

The woman took Brett's name and number and assured him that she would call if anything turned up.

Brett knew what he had to do. Maria Russo was back in Tony's home town of Fiesole, Italy, and the only way to talk to her was to go there.

He threw on a pair of shorts and a t-shirt along with some sandals and drove down to his office. Piled at least two feet high next to his desk was a stack of dental journals from the last six months. One by one he started to leaf through them. After forty-five minutes he found what he was looking for. Two weeks from now in Florence, Italy, the International Academy of Implant Dentistry was holding its annual conference.

He dialed up Annie's number. "Hello."

"Annie, it's me, I have a great idea. It might be a chance for you to get away from the house and enjoy yourself for a week."

"What's your idea?"

"Have you had breakfast yet?"

"No, why?"

"Meet me in a half hour at Max's in Redwood City. I'll buy you breakfast and pitch my idea."

Annie had a little trepidation in her voice but said, "Okay, I'll see you there."

Brett was in a corner booth drinking a cup of coffee and finishing the *Chronicle* when Annie slipped in next to him. She was wearing an orange and black baseball cap with a SF logo and a tee shirt that said GIANTS on the front. Brett looked up from his newspaper. "I thought you hated baseball. Since when have you been a fan?"

"I haven't had much to do lately, so I've been watching the games on TV. It looks like they may make the playoffs."

Brett thought he'd test her. "Who do they have that's hitting?"

She was ready. "Well, Bonds and Kent are the big guns, but Mueller and Aurilia are really banging the ball."

"I'm impressed. What looks good for breakfast?" Brett replied.

Max's menu was huge and had portions to match. "I can't eat one of these breakfasts by myself. You wanna split?" Annie said.

"Sure, pick an omelet but no spinach."

Annie did the ordering and then looked Brett square in the eye. "Okay, you didn't get me down here just to split an omelet. What's your great idea?"

"Well, I'm toying with the idea of going to an implant conference in Italy two weeks from Monday. You need something more to look forward to than a Giant's game. How about you coming along, go to a few museums, maybe do some shopping."

Annie thought for a moment. "Brett I think it's a great idea for you to go, but you don't need to drag along your ex-wife."

"Twenty years ago we looked through a travel magazine and pledged that one day we'd go to Italy. I know this isn't how we dreamed it, but at least we'll be there together. The entire trip will only be a week."

"I don't know, somehow it doesn't seem right."

"Annie, I'm not going to pressure you. I really do want you to come along, and I honestly think you'd enjoy it, but do what makes you feel comfortable."

Down deep she wanted to go. "If I go I'm not letting you pay for me, I'm already sucking $4,000 a month from your bank account."

Brett could feel her softening. "We'll negotiate that issue."

"It's non-negotiable. I just came into five million dollars; I think I can afford to pay my own way."

Brett knew he had her. "Okay, it's a deal." He stuck out his hand.

After leaving Max's, Brett dropped in at a travel agency he knew was open on Saturday. Two weeks was very short notice for a trip to Europe in the summer. All the flights to Rome and Milan were full; however, the agent located two tickets from San Francisco to Zurich. There was only one flight from Zurich to Florence and it was fully booked, so she arranged for a rental car that could be picked up in Switzerland and dropped off in Italy.

Knowing that a road trip from Zurich to Florence, after getting off an eleven hour flight, would be pushing the envelope, the agent arranged for two rooms in a small hotel at Lake Lugano, a gorgeous spot on the border between Switzerland and Italy. The next day Brett and Annie would drive to Florence, where she booked them into a five star hotel.

The trip home was no problem. The travel agent was able to get a flight out of Florence later in the week which would get them to Milan, where there was space open on a direct flight back to San Francisco.

Chapter Sixteen

Brett made a point to get to the office an hour earlier on Monday morning. He knew Ginger would be there. She was twelve years older than Brett and fancied herself as his surrogate mother. Ginger loved the office and she loved Brett. If they went into battle together, she would take a bullet for him.

Brett walked in through the office entrance and Ginger was already there. "Morning Ginger."

She looked up. "Well, well, what brings the good doctor to the office an hour early on a Monday morning?"

"Let's grab a cup of coffee and talk in my office."

"It sounds like I'm getting fired."

"There's no way I could fire you. I'm always worried you're going to fire me."

Brett sat in his desk chair and Ginger pulled up the recliner Brett uses to cat nap in during his breaks. "You're going to have to cancel another week out of my appointment book."

"Dr. Raven, you're kidding. I had to cancel a week for that Mexico trip."

"Ginger, I want you to call me Dr. Raven in front of patients and staff, but, when we're alone, couldn't you just call me Brett?"

Ginger blushed a little. "I guess I could, but it seems awkward."

"Well give it a try, you probably know me better than anyone other than my ex-wife."

She blushed again. "Okay Dr..., Brett, I'll try. So why do I need to cancel?"

"I'm going to Italy for a week."

"I don't get it, why the traveling all of a sudden?"

Brett's tone became very serious. "Ginger, you're the only one I can trust to tell this to. I don't want anyone else to know, not even Annie."

Ginger didn't speak.

"J.T.'s death wasn't an accident, I know it. I can't give you the details, but suffice it to say I'm on the track of finding out the answer."

Ginger's face displayed alarm. "Oh my God, are you saying he was murdered?"

"That's what I suspect."

"B.... Brett, are you in danger?"

"I doubt it. Not just yet anyway."

The mother in Ginger came out. "You have to tell the police. Let them handle it, then you won't be in harm's way."

"It's not so simple. I need to find out more

facts. That's why I went to Mexico and that's the reason for the trip to Italy."

"I guess I was right. You didn't walk into a hotel room wall to get that black eye, did you?"

Brett moved the conversation back to the Italy trip. "I've invited Annie to go along with me. She needs to get away from her place for awhile. I told her I was going to a convention in Florence, but I'm really going to interview someone. She can't know anything about this."

"Oh Brett, I'm so happy you're taking her with you. Is their any chance the two of you might get back together?"

Brett sat and reflected. "Ginger, I've fantasized about it, but I'm afraid. There's been a lot of water spilled over this dam. If I try to scoop it back in, I'm afraid I'll fail, and if I do, it would be the end of our friendship forever. I'd rather have Annie as just a friend, than not have her at all."

Ginger got tears in her eyes. "I understand, but I can still hope." She wiped the corners of her eyes with a Kleenex from her pocket. "Okay, I'll cancel the week. Which one?"

"Two weeks from today."

Ginger got up to leave. "Consider it done."

Brett got up to open the door. "I may be asking for some more help in the next month or so. Maybe, when it's over, I can tell you all about it, but don't count on it."

"I understand, be careful, please."

Brett opened the door. "Thanks Ginger, I will."

Chapter Seventeen

The flight from San Francisco to Zurich was scheduled to leave at five p.m. With the eight hour time difference and the eleven hour flight, they would arrive in Switzerland around noon the next day.

Sunday evening Brett gave Annie a call. "Hi, Annie. It's me, are you packed?"

"There's not that much to pack. I figure we'll be two days in travel, so packing for about five nights should do it."

Brett felt a little guilty. "Yeah, I guess I should have taken more time off."

"Hey, I'm not complaining. As a matter of fact I've been counting the hours till we leave."

"That's great, how about I pick you up at two thirty?"

"I'll be ready, see you then."

"See ya."

Because Brett had gotten the tickets so late, they were seated in the back side row of the plane. It actually worked out well. There were only two seats in the row and as soon as dinner was over, they each popped an Ambien, leaned their shoulders together and managed to get six hours of sleep.

Brett signed for the rental car, a compact Opel with a manual gearshift. Annie threw their two small bags in the back seat and they headed south toward Italy. It was only ninety-six miles from Zurich to Lugano; however, they were told with the heavy traffic around Zurich, it would take at least an hour to get out of the city. Brett figured even with jet lag, he could handle two and half hours behind the wheel.

The travel agent had booked a small three star, the Hotel Nassa Garni, located away from the center of town and overlooking Lake Lugano. Brett pulled the car into the hotel parking lot at ten minutes to four.

The hotel was quaint with its small lobby and antique furniture. Brett registered and handed Annie a key. "We have rooms right next to each other on the third floor facing the lake."

Annie hadn't asked about the sleeping arrangements and wasn't surprised they would have separate rooms. "Thanks, I hope I don't hear you snoring through the wall. As I recall you can really saw a log when you sleep."

"I was hoping you might have forgotten

that. Let's clean up and meet for a drink in an hour."

A narrow street separated the hotel from the lake; however, the hotel had an outdoor bar and lounge that sat right on the shore. A little traffic dodging and Brett and Annie were seated right next to the water.

They each ordered a glass of red wine and sat quietly taking in the scenery. The lake was deep blue, surrounded by Swiss mountains on the north and Italian mountains to the south. The foothills were dotted with houses displaying red tile roofs giving Brett and Annie the impression they were looking at a painting rather than a real scene.

Annie was the first to speak. "I looked at the map and we're actually still in Switzerland. We don't enter Italy until we're about five miles down the highway. Since we'll be eating Italian for the next few days, let's order Swiss tonight."

"Go for it." Brett replied as he sampled the red wine.

They each had a salad and split a huge portion of their favorite veal dish, Wienerschnitzel, along with a plate of Rosti.

It was only eight o'clock, but they were both exhausted. They agreed to meet for breakfast and get started for Florence by nine the next morning.

They were on the road by nine-thirty. Most of the trip was spent on the Italian Freeway system, the Autostrade, allowing the hundred and ninety miles to slip by in less than three hours. The entrance to the city was magnificent. The highway dropped from the Tuscan hills down into the valley where the city was located with its skyline of old churches and museums.

They drove across the Arno, a gorgeous river separating Florence into north and south, and pulled up in front of the Hotel Lungarno. The hotel was very old; however, it was elegant and obviously had been remodeled to earn the five star rating it now boasted. The lobby was done in dark wood with tile floors; one side faced the river while the other had a view of the Florence skyline.

Brett registered with the desk clerk, turned the car in and gestured to a bellman to take their luggage. The bellman directed them to their sixth floor suite. Brett had decided on a suite, so that they could be together without any awkward situation regarding sleeping arrangements. The entry opened into a living room furnished with a couch, two chairs and a coffee table. Two sliding glass doors opened onto a terrace with a view of the city. To the right of the living room was a small bedroom and bath, and on the left was a spacious master with a large bathroom.

Brett looked into the master bedroom and then into the smaller one. "Annie, why don't you take the big room? I'll be fine with this one."

"No way, this is your trip, I'm just here as an extra." Before he could protest, Annie had taken possession of the smaller room.

The next morning Brett and Annie had breakfast

at a table overlooking the river. Brett had decided he would at least register for the conference and check out the speakers. "I'm headed over to the conference. Are you alright on your own?"

"Come on Brett, we already agreed, I don't need a baby sitter. I brought three credit cards, I'll be busy."

"Sorry, just checking. I'll see you back here for dinner."

Brett returned to the hotel in the early afternoon. He sat down at the desk of the concierge and made a request. "I want to visit a family in Fiesole. Their name is Russo, could you help me locate their address?"

The attractive young lady gave Brett a wide smile and said. "The name Russo in Italy is like the name Smith in your country. There are probably dozens of families with that name in Fiesole. Let's check"

The concierge pulled out a telephone directory and started counting. "There are eighty-four Russo's in Florence and the surrounding communities. Let me count how many in Fiesole." She took a pen and started down the list. Behind each address that had Fis... after it she placed a check mark. She looked up at Brett. "There are twenty-four Russo's in Fiesole."

Brett hadn't anticipated this problem. "Could you make me a copy of those pages with the addresses?"

"Certainly." The young lady said as she went to the copy machine.

Brett took the list and stuffed it into his pocket. "Could I ask another favor? I need a car for tomorrow with a driver who speaks English and knows the streets in Fiesole."

"That's no problem, what time should he be here?"

"How about ten o'clock?"

"He'll meet you here in the lobby."

Brett thanked the young lady and went back to his room to prepare for his meeting with Maria.

Over breakfast the next day Brett and Annie planned their day. Brett was going to make the trip to the Russo house; however, he couldn't let Annie know. Instead he said, "I'll probably be at the implant conference all day. Do you still have shopping to do?"

"This is a shopoholic's paradise; I'll be busy all day."

"The conference should be over by four, I'll meet you back here about four thirty for a drink."

The driver was in the lobby right on time at ten o'clock. Brett handed him the list with the twenty-four check marks. "Let's start at the top. I have to visit every address until I find the family I'm looking for."

It only took the driver fifteen minutes to navigate the windy road into the hills above Florence. As he entered the village he passed by remains of the original wall which was built around Fiesole nine hundred years before Christ.

One by one Brett went to the door of a Russo

family. At each house he said, "mi scusi, sto cercando Maria Russo." The first thirteen stops all ended with the same result. No Maria Russo lived there.

The driver pulled to a stop in front of a small house squeezed in close proximity to the ones on either side. The outside was covered with white plaster turning brown from the ivy staining it, as the plant climbed toward the roof. Pieces had begun to chip from the exterior walls revealing red bricks underneath.

Brett walked up the short cobblestone walkway and knocked on the door. A dog started to bark and he could hear someone coming toward the door yelling, "Dante, silenzio, Dante, silenzio." The door opened and a good looking man about forty-five years old smiled at him and said, "Saluto."

"Saluto" Brett replied. "Mi scusi, do you speak any English?"

"Si, a little."

"I'm from the U.S. Does a Maria Russo live here?'

"Si, Maria live here."

Are you by any chance Tony's brother?"

"Si, I am his brother, Sergio."

Brett gave a sigh of relief. "Sergio, may I come in?"

"Entrare, entrare."

The young man turned toward the kitchen. "Mama, mama, due expresso per favore."

Sergio pointed to a small couch which was

covered by a multi colored knit afghan.

"You are a friend of Tony's, yes?"

Brett was feeling a little uncomfortable. "Well, actually we have a mutual friend. He gave me the address here in Fiesole."

"Si, si, Tony no here now."

Brett tried to show his sympathy. "Yes I know. I actually came to speak with Maria, if she's here."

In rapid response to Sergio's request to the kitchen, a little old lady pushed through a swinging wood door carrying a tray with two small coffee cups and a pot of what Brett reasoned was filled with espresso. The woman was only about four foot eight and was stooped over at the waist from the hard work of the last eighty years. Her hair was pure white and tied into a bun in the back. She wore a faded housedress, hemmed below her knees, and rolled down to just above her black laced shoes, were her thick brown stockings.

The old lady set the coffee down and Sergio said, "Mama, this man from the U.S. has a friend who know Tony. He would like to talk to you."

Brett was dumbfounded. "Sergio, I'm so sorry, I wanted to talk to Tony's wife, Maria."

Sergio laughed. "Last time I see Tony, he not married. He been traveling the world for over a year now. Knowing Tony he could have wife, but we wouldn't know until he return."

Brett didn't know what to say. It was apparent Tony had left Italy over a year ago and his family didn't know he had married. Worse yet, they didn't know he had been killed in a plane crash. He couldn't tell them. A stranger couldn't just show up on their doorstep with that kind of news.

"Sergio, I have to apologize to you and your mother. I guess someone gave me the wrong information. He got up to leave. "I hope you hear from Tony, thanks for the coffee."

"No problem. I tell Tony you were here, when he return."

Brett shook hands with Sergio and walked back to the car. He was stunned and would have to sort it out later. Even though his mind wasn't on dentistry, he felt he should make another appearance at the conference and had the driver drop him off there.

He left the conference at four o'clock and decided to walk back to the Lungarno. In order to reach the hotel he had to walk across the Ponte Vecchio, Florence's most famous old bridge which crosses the Arno River. The entire bridge is lined with shops and stalls where merchants sell artwork, personal crafts, expensive jewelry and tourist junk.

As Brett worked his way through the crowds on the bridge he spotted Annie talking to the owner of an upscale jewelry shop. He inched in behind her without letting her know he was there. She was looking at a bracelet that Brett could see was unique and one of a kind.

It was constructed with three different colors of gold: yellow, white and rose. The surface was done in the Florentine style which gave it the look of lace, a technique originated in the city hundreds of years ago. It was about a half inch wide, and hinged in the middle with a clasp at the end. The bracelet was extremely feminine and Brett could see it was a piece of art.

He slipped away without Annie seeing him and met her back in the hotel bar a half hour later. "I ordered Martini's. Tanqueray up, very dry, with the olives on the side."

Annie felt the liquid warm her throat and chest as she swallowed it. "How was the conference?"

"Really interesting," he lied. "How was shopping?

"Nothing interesting," she lied.

Brett popped an olive in his mouth. "It's only six o'clock and nobody eats in this town until at least nine. I asked the concierge, and she suggested we walk a block down the street to a place called Mama Gina's. They'll tolerate our strange American eating customs."

They had a simple Italian dinner of insalata mista, followed by cheese tortellini with ragu. On the walk back to the hotel Brett said, "I want to skip the conference tomorrow. How about we go sight seeing?"

Brett, you're here for the conference, you don't have to look after me."

"I realize I can talk about teeth anytime, but neither one of us may ever get back to Florence again. This is a dream we had twenty years ago, let's do it."

Annie looked pleased. "We better wear our running shoes. I have the feeling we're going to need them."

Florence is a Mecca for people who love museums, artwork, sculpture and churches. Brett and Annie started at the Galleria dell' Accademia. They had to stand in line for an hour and fifteen minutes, but it was worth it. They were able to see Michelangelo's world famous marble sculpture of David, as well as Botticelli's painting, Madonna and Child. When their feet began to ache, they decided to take a break and found a place to sit in a nearby piazza.

Brett had stopped at a gelato stand and he handed Annie a cone containing the icy rich chocolate. "One museum down and a hundred left to go."

Annie took a big lick from the gelato. "It's not the museums that are tiring; it's the waiting in line."

"I agree, but we have to see a couple more."

They made their way to the most famous museum in Florence, the Uffizi Gallery. The line was listed as a two hour wait. Brett spied a private tour going past the waiting lines. He grabbed Annie's hand and pulled her into the group, hiding her between two, three hundred pound women from Iowa. Annie was laughing so hard she almost blew the deal. Inside walked the tour group along with Brett and his hysterical companion.

They both were getting tired, but agreed to spend an hour in the Leonardo Museum. After all one couldn't visit Italy and not take in the works of da Vinci.

On the way back to the Lungarno they stepped into a wine shop where Brett bought two bottles of a Chianti Classico, and two bottles of a Pinot Grigio.

It was almost seven o'clock by the time Brett and Annie got back to their hotel room. Brett gave out a sigh. "I'm exhausted. How about we stay here, clean up, and have some dinner sent up?"

"I was thinking the same thing. You can be in charge of the dinner; I'm headed for a hot tub."

"Take your time I'll meet you out on the terrace in an hour."

Brett looked over the menu and made a call to room service. He uncorked a bottle of the Pinot Grigio and placed it inside an ice bucket on the coffee table. Then he made a bee line for a hot shower.

After his shower Brett slipped on his pajama shorts with no top, and put on the white monogrammed hotel bathrobe. He went into the living room, picked up the bottle of wine and poured himself a glass. He knew Annie would take another half hour, so he took the bottle with him and went out on the terrace. He sipped the wine while he pieced together the information he had obtained yesterday.

He had struck out. The reason he had come to Florence was to meet Tony's widow, Maria. He needed to find out why Tony had come back to the

U.S., why he had re-connected with J.T, and what he was doing on that trip to Baja. Instead he found that Tony left Italy a year ago and had never told his family of his marriage to Maria. Worse yet, Tony's family doesn't even know he's dead.

Annie dried herself and gazed into the mirror. She looked pretty good for forty two years old. Never having children had left her stomach flat and her breasts quite firm. Her legs hadn't changed; they still showed subtle muscle definition in the thighs and calves. She only weighed a hundred and ten pounds, just ten more than when she had first met Brett twenty four years ago. She wasn't a sun lover so her skin was still smooth and very few wrinkles were on her face. Her hair wasn't much different from her college style; it was still short; however, now it was highlighted with a little blond.

Annie dabbed a touch of Opium behind her ears and between her breasts and looked for something to put on. She was never a nightgown type of woman. In the top drawer she located the pair of silk pajamas she had bought at Saks two days before the trip. They were exquisite. The silk was off-white and had embroidery along the button line. The top had only three buttons, all covered by fabric. The bottoms were very plain but had a silk drawstring that ruffled them along the waist. She put them on and took the bathrobe from behind the door and wrapped it around her as she headed for the terrace.

Brett was on his second glass, when Annie settled into the chair next to him. "White wine?" Brett asked.

"I'd love it."

Annie took the glass and they both were silent as they looked over the Florence skyline. Annie studied Brett and reflected how different he looked from the day they were married. He had put on twenty five pounds, but they had filled out his face and chest, giving him a nice mature look. He still wore his hair a little long to cover the tops of his ears; however, gray was beginning to appear around his temples. His face, as usual, was tan, making his teeth look even whiter than they were.

The silence began to get uncomfortable. Brett started up with small talk. "What did you think of the David?"

"His hands are too big and his penis is too small."

Brett broke out laughing. He realized he hadn't heard Annie crack a joke in six years. He missed her.

The sun was setting over Florence and the water of the Arno was reflecting the orange color from the lights of the city as it started to come alive. There was a knock at the door. Brett went to open it and motioned the waiter with the table of food toward the terrace. The waiter rolled the table through the living room and situated it between the two chairs on the terrace. Brett signed the check and the waiter slipped out the door.

He removed the silver lid from the dish in front of him and offered Annie some fried calamari which she dipped in a spicy aioli. "Did you plan the menu or did you leave it up to the kitchen?" Annie asked.

"I've had to learn a lot about food these last five years. It's been different without a woman in the house."

When the squid was almost gone, Brett uncovered a dish of pappardelle. He put a small portion on each plate and spooned some of the mushroom sauce on top. He opened another bottle of Pinot Grigio and topped off their glasses. They sat in silence, while they rolled the pasta onto their forks, until Annie spoke. "I feel I have to apologize."

Brett knew what was coming. "Annie, don't go there. You have nothing to apologize for."

"I didn't try to save our marriage. I was so damned consumed with grief and anger. I was angry at you for pushing me into that abortion back when we were in college, and I was angry at myself for being too weak to fight you."

Brett reached across the table and put his hand over hers. "Annie, I'm so ashamed of how selfish I was twenty years ago. I always felt I could make it up to you, but when you had the miscarriage I knew I never could. I don't blame you for wanting the divorce."

Annie put her other hand on top of his. "I wanted to show you I could make my own decisions."

Annie withdrew her hands and peaked under the large serving dish. The smell of braised rabbit filled her nostrils. Brett went to the bar and selected two large wine glasses. He pulled the cork off a bottle of Chianti Classico, poured the glasses half full and sat back down at the table.

Annie broke the silence again. "You were right about my marriage to J.T. It was never a fit, it was a convenience. I didn't want to be alone and he needed to pretend he could be a happily married man. We both were fooling ourselves." A couple tears dropped off her cheeks.

"Hey Annie, you're dripping saltwater all over the rabbit, you're diluting the sauce."

Annie smiled and wiped her eyes with her napkin. "Sorry, I'm getting all sappy. I know you hate sappy."

Brett smiled back and topped off their wine glasses while they finished up the rabbit. After the last spoonful of sauce was gone, he flipped the lid on the silver carafe, poured some espresso into the small cups, and portioned out the tiramisu from its chilled dish.

He sat back and waited for Annie to pick up the conversation. "I've been so lonely the last couple years. J.T. traveled two weeks out of every month and, when he was home, we grew more and more distant. We never joked around and laughed the way you and I always did. He was always so serious. Money was everything to him, and his fear of losing it obsessed him."

"Why didn't you tell me?"

"I had already hurt you enough and we really

weren't communicating. I didn't want to call you out of the blue and load more baggage on your shoulders."

Brett leaned over and placed his lips on Annie's. He let them linger for a second or two and then pulled away. "I can't tell you how much those birthday cards meant to me. I've always remembered the good times too."

The moon had risen over the city and the lights were flickering like thousands of fire flies in the distance. Annie wanted to ask Brett a question, but she turned away afraid of the answer. "Can I sleep in your bed tonight?"

Brett was silent for a few moments. "Annie, are you sure you want to do that? If it doesn't work, it could ruin the relationship we're still clinging to."

Now she looked directly at Brett. "You're going to have to accept the fact that I'm no longer that eighteen year old you met at the fraternity party. I'm forty-two years old, I know what I want, and I want to spend tonight with you."

Brett had a surprised look that quickly faded into a warm smile. "Do you have an extra pillow? You know I need two for myself."

Annie returned Brett's smile. "I'll bring one with me."

While Brett was in the bathroom Annie took off her robe, dimmed the light and slid under the covers. Brett opened the door and could see the outline of Annie's head on the pillow.

He dropped his robe on the floor and slipped

under the covers. It had been five years, since they had shared a bed. Brett nudged close and put his arms around her. His nostrils filled with the sweet aroma of Opium perfume, the same scent she had worn in their college years.

He stroked her back through the silk pajamas. The silk was smooth and his hands moved easily and slowly from her shoulders to her waist. She put her arms around Brett's naked back and began stroking to the same rhythm.

Brett felt Annie trembling. He lifted his head, "Are you nervous?"

She opened her eyes, "I think I am."

Brett grinned, "So am I."

They began to giggle and the giggling turned into laughter. They laughed until tears came to their eyes. Finally, Brett leaned down and placed his lips on hers.

He undid the three silk covered buttons and eased Annie out of her pajama top. Now their chests were bare and touching and Annie could feel his hair against her breasts. He caressed her left breast and then cradling the nipple between his thumb and forefinger he gently pinched the skin. As it began to get hard, he kissed his way down and took it between his lips, teasing the tip with his tongue.

Annie's nails dug into Brett's back as he ran his fingers down her silk pajamas. She spread her legs slightly to allow his hand to slide in between and he began caressing through the silk. He could feel her dampness permeate the fabric beneath his fingers.

Suddenly she felt the crackle of static electricity as he kept rubbing the silk against her skin. She began to breathe hard, gave a shudder, and then she was still.

Minutes passed before Annie began kissing Brett's chest as she undid the drawstring of his shorts and dropped them beneath his feet. He felt oven hot to her delicate hand as she began to massage while rolling him onto his back.

Annie's fingers felt Brett's response. She slithered out of her pajama bottoms, rose to her knees, and straddled him in an upright position. He gripped her shoulders and drew her down to him. She kissed him hard and bit his lip until the salty taste of blood hit her tongue. She withdrew from the kiss and pushed his arms behind his head pinning them down with her elbows.

Slowly she moved her hips up and down. He struggled to get his arms free to wrap around her, but before he could, he exploded. As he relaxed, Annie's body began to shudder once again and a deep moan escaped as she let free of his arms. Brett put them behind Annie's neck and pulled her mouth to his. They remained in the embrace until their breathing returned to normal.

Annie rolled off Brett and lay beside him. Brett buried his lips against her neck and gently kissed her over and over again. He leaned toward her ear and softly said, "I love you so much." To his surprise, all he could hear was her deep breathing. She was asleep and hadn't heard his whisper.

The morning light came shining through the drapes. Brett pulled himself out of bed and found the robe he had dropped on the floor the night before. He walked into the living room and spotted Annie sitting on the terrace. Last night's dishes had been cleared away and in their place were a pot of coffee and a basket of croissants.

"Coffee?" Annie asked.

"Please." Brett replied as he settled into the same chair as last night. "Was it for real or was it just the wine?"

"Believe me it was real, but let's not start analyzing it. I'm afraid if we do, it will ruin it."

After they finished off the pastry, Brett emptied the last drop of coffee from his cup and said, "We need to be at the airport by two. We have a couple hours. Go take a shower, there's something I want to show you before we leave."

They strolled down the Arno toward the Ponte Vecchio. When they reached the bridge Brett casually walked up to the jewelry shop where Annie had seen the Florentine bracelet. "Hey Annie, come look, this bracelet would look great on you."

Annie came over and immediately recognized it from the day before yesterday. The price tag was $3,000. She could have bought it for herself and she certainly didn't want Brett to buy it for her. She picked it up and said, "Not my style."

Brett flipped his American Express on the

counter and said to the owner. "I'll take it anyway. It would look great on a special lady I know."

When they got back to their suite Brett took Annie's wrist and clasped the bracelet in place. Annie smiled and said, "Am I your special lady now?"

Brett softly put his lips on Annie's neck. "You always have been."

Chapter Eighteen

Monday morning Brett was ready to get back to his office. He had postponed treatment for too many patients, a policy which went against his basic practice philosophy. As he shaved and showered he thought about the trip to Italy. He hadn't found Maria; however, he had found Annie. Unfortunately neither one of them was yet ready to discuss the night they had spent together at the Lungarno. Brett wasn't in a hurry. He knew both of them had to determine what it really meant.

Brett got to the office an hour early and sure enough Ginger was already there. "Behold the world traveler. How did it go?"

"Hi Ginger, good and bad."

Ginger winced. "Let's hear the good first."

"Annie and I had a wonderful time together. It was like old times."

"Oh Dr. Rav.., I mean Brett. Goddamn I can't

get used to that. What does it mean?"

"Who knows; I think we pushed a little water back in the dam."

"That is good news, what's the bad news?"

Brett had a dejected look. "My interview was non-existent, a dead end."

"That's too bad. While you were gone, you received a phone call from Minneapolis. I thought it might be important, so I put it on the top of your mail."

Brett had an immediate mood swing. "Thanks Ginger. I've been hoping for that call."

He disappeared into his private office. The message was on top of the stack of mail, just as Ginger had said.

> *Mrs. Janway called from Minneapolis. She has found four boxes that were left behind. Please call her. 612-958-2376.*

Brett's patients were starting to arrive and there was no time to place the phone call. After being away for a week, he was swamped and lunch was out of the question; instead he went into the lounge for a five minute break and a cup of coffee with a doughnut. Annie was getting ready for lunch.

"Hi Brett, any jet lag?"

"Yeah, I think it takes about a week. How 'bout you?"

"Not bad, but I don't have to sweat over patients like you do."

"Annie we had a wonderful time together in Italy,

can we get together and talk about it pretty soon?"

"I think we should, but right now your reception room is bulging with patients. You better get going."

Brett scarfed down the doughnut and took a gulp from the coffee cup. "I have to get back, how about dinner tonight?"

"Great. Pick me up at seven?"

"Will do." And he was gone.

Brett worked straight through from eight to five-thirty. He was tired, but he knew Minneapolis was two hours ahead of the west coast and he had to get back to Mrs. Janway before it was too late to call.

He dialed 612-958-2376. A female voice answered. "Hello"

"Hello, Mrs. Janway?"

"Yes."

"This is Brett Raven in California. I'm sorry I'm late getting back to you, but I was out of the country."

"Oh yes, Dr. Raven, your receptionist told me it would be a few days. We finally got all of our boxes unpacked and low and behold there were four left over that didn't belong to us."

Brett's adrenalin started to flow. "I assume Maria Russo left them behind."

"They must be hers, because they're not ours, but frankly, they look like a lot of junk."

Brett still felt that this was a stroke of good luck. "I understand, but I'd like to pick them up anyway. I could be in Minneapolis next Monday, would that be convenient?"

"That would be fine. I'll be home all day. Do you have our address?"

"I do thanks. I understand you're out at Lake Minnetonka. I'll get directions at the rental car agency. See you next Monday."

"See you then, goodbye."

Ginger was getting ready to leave for the day when Brett called her on the intercom. "Ginger, could I talk to you for a minute?"

"Oh no, am I getting fired again?"

"Yeah, get in here."

Ginger knocked on the door and walked in before getting a response. "Don't say it; you're not going to be here next week."

Brett laughed. She had a sixth sense. "Only for one day. Cancel next Monday; I'll work my day off on Friday to make up for it."

"Okay, I'll tell them Sherlock Holmes won't be here on Monday."

Brett didn't get back to the townhouse until six fifteen but had time to run through a quick shower. He pulled on a pair of jeans with a silk tee shirt and headed down to Atherton.

Annie met him at the door and jumped into the Porsche. "Jeez, Brett, you look wiped out."

"I'm fine, just a little tired."

"You want to scratch the restaurant? I'll make some scrambled eggs."

"Would you mind?"

Annie knew Brett was exhausted, and not just physically, she sensed he was emotionally spent. "Come on in and make us drinks, while I whip up some food."

Brett felt a wave of relief. He followed her inside, went to the bar and poured two glasses of Scotch. He brought them into the kitchen and handed one to Annie.

Annie took a taste and looked up at Brett. "What's wrong, Brett? I know something's bothering you."

Brett hated having to lie to Annie again, but he wasn't going to share his burden with her. "I'm fine really. I just found out a classmate of mine in Minneapolis died from a sudden heart attack. I have to go back Sunday for the funeral."

"Oh, I'm so sorry. Is it anyone I'd remember?"

"I don't think so; he was kind of a loner. I'm taking a flight Sunday morning and I'll be back by Monday night."

Annie put the eggs and toast on the table and they washed them down with the scotch. "Brett you're too tired to get into a heavy discussion tonight, so let's table it; I want you to know how wonderful the trip to Italy was for me, and I don't just mean the night of romance; although it wasn't too bad either."

Brett smiled. "No, it wasn't too bad, was it?"

Annie went silent for a minute then said, "Just answer one question. You're a great catch for a woman. Why haven't you gotten involved over these last five years?"

Brett closed his eyes and then opened them. "I've been involved and had a couple serious relationships, but honestly Annie, I've never gotten over you."

Brett got up from the table and Annie walked him to the door. She kissed him on the lips. "Goodnight, Brett."

"Goodnight, Annie."

Chapter Nineteen

Brett caught a Northwest flight out of San Francisco at noon on Sunday. Minneapolis was two hours ahead putting his arrival at five ten.

He picked up a rental car and drove to the Embassy Suites, located about a half hour from Lake Minnetonka. He got a good night's sleep and headed out to the Janway residence at nine Monday morning.

Mrs. Janway was very gracious and invited him in for coffee. He declined. "You said that Maria left four boxes?"

"Yes, come in, they're in the garage."

Mrs. Janway led him to the garage and pointed to four dilapidated cardboard boxes.

"They look like they went through a world war. Why don't I just throw them in the trunk and go through them at the hotel? If there's anything of value, I'll see that Maria gets it."

Mrs. Janway looked relieved. "That's fine, I'm glad to get rid of them."

Brett put the boxes in the trunk of the rental, thanked Mrs. Janway and drove back to the hotel.

He parked in the hotel lot and poured the first box upside down on the pavement. All that came out was a lot of junk; old hair curlers, two year old Glamour magazines and other useless items. The next two boxes were equally unproductive. By now the pile in the parking lot was getting embarrassing, and people were walking by muttering unflattering comments.

When Brett dumped the last box upside down, one item caught his eye. Amongst the junk was a rather attractive handbag. He extracted it from the pile and opened the clasp. The contents looked disappointing: a pack of Doublemint gum, some Kleenex, two quarters and a nickel. He was getting ready to toss it in the pile, when he noticed a business card stuck to the bottom of the purse. He wiped some hair off the card and examined it. It was actually an appointment card for a local dentist.

Most of it was pre-printed, but it had the name Maria, the date Feb 6th, and the time 10 a.m. penciled in the blanks. On the bottom it read:

Ralph Williamson D.D.S.

122 W. Cedar Lake Parkway

Minneapolis, Minn. 67507

612-555-7155

Brett scooped up the trash pile he had created

and deposited it in the dumpster at the end of the parking lot. He went to the front desk and inquired where he might find an office supply store; he was directed to a Staples six blocks away. Brett found the store and perused the aisles finally deciding on a pack of heavy stock, beige, 3 x 5 blank cards.

He drove to a shopping mall two blocks away and located a store which sold luggage and leather goods. He wanted a wallet designed for the sole purpose of identification; they had one. It was made of black leather and was about five inches high and three inches wide. When opened, it revealed a plastic covered pocket inside the front cover and another inside the back cover. There were no other pockets in the wallet. He bought it along with a cheap black briefcase and headed back to his hotel.

The Embassy Suites where Brett was staying catered to businessmen and women. On the main floor off the corner of the lobby was a large room called the Business Center. It housed half a dozen desks, each supporting a desktop computer and a telephone. Near the rear of the room, the hotel had supplied two color printers, a fax machine, a scanner, a paper cutter, and a shredder. Seated near the door was an attendant, who was there to help with the use of the equipment.

Brett asked the attendant, if she could link up one of the computers to a scanner and a printer. What Brett thought would be a complicated task, the young lady accomplished in less than five minutes.

Brett picked up the phone and called his office. Ginger answered with her usual professional and friendly greeting. Brett said, "Ginger, it's me, could you do me a favor?"

"Oh, Brett, of course. What is it?"

"In the top drawer of the desk in my private office there's a letter from the National Transportation Safety Board. Would you fax it to me at 615-555-2300?"

"It'll be there in twenty minutes. Are you going to make it home by tomorrow morning? You have patients scheduled from eight-thirty on."

"I'll be there, see you tomorrow."

The fax arrived in less than ten minutes and the quality was incredibly clear. Apparently the hotel didn't skimp on their office equipment. He put the letter through the scanner and moved it onto the computer he was using. Then he highlighted only the logo and the letterhead and dropped them on to a separate page. He went to EDIT and then PAGE SETUP and arranged the margins of the document to a 3 x 5 format. The page was reduced; across the top it read, **National Transportation Safety Board**, followed by the logo. An inch below the letterhead Brett typed the name, **Frank Dillon—Special Agent**. He then went back to the scanner, placed his California Driver's license into the machine, and transferred the images to his computer. He extracted only his picture and pasted it below the name.

He asked the attendant again for help. He

didn't know how to fit the 3 x 5 cards into the printer. It only took the young lady about three keystrokes and a tray adjustment to accomplish the task.

Brett placed six of the 3 x 5 heavy cards that he had purchased in the printer and pressed PRINT. The first card came out too light and his picture didn't look right. He changed to a darker print and ran it again. Something still gave the look of an amateur job to the document. Brett studied it for about ten minutes and then changed the contrast to MAX, and ran it again. "That looks pretty good," Brett mumbled to himself.

After pushing the first two trial cards through the shredder, he took the final copy to the paper cutter and sliced off an eighth of an inch from all sides of the card. He smudged the surface with a little dust from under the desk, and he slipped the card under the plastic inside the front cover of the leather wallet. "Wow," he said.

Brett was a member of the San Mateo County Sheriff Air Squadron at the San Carlos Airport. It's a group of volunteer pilots who aid the Sheriff with search and rescue as well as surveillance of criminal activity. The pilots weren't paid anything; however, as a perk, they were all given the same gold badges the deputies carry. The first time it came in handy was when Brett was stopped on the 280 freeway for going ninety-two mph in his Porsche. When the highway patrolman saw the badge inside his wallet, he cut him some slack and let him off with a warning.

This would be the second time the badge would come in handy. He took it out of his money wallet and placed it under the plastic inside the back cover of the new black ID wallet. The plastic blurred the lettering enough that it would take careful examination to determine which agency it represented. Brett admired his work. "Hello special agent Frank Dillon of the NTSB."

His preparation wasn't quite finished. He changed the margins for the setup of a new document. This one he set for 2 x 4. He again transferred the NTSB letter head and logo to the document. Underneath he placed the name Frank Dillon, Special Agent. He put another six 3 x 5 cards into the printer and ran them through. When they were finished, he went to the paper cutter. Using one of the business cards from his dental practice as a template, he made perfect cuts which left him with six new business cards.

Brett had only brought jeans and a sport shirt on this trip and now he needed to look more professional. Six blocks from the hotel he found a Mens Wearhouse. Brett was pretty close to a perfect thirty-nine coat and his waist was still at thirty-two. He bought a blue suit off the rack and the tailor in the store had the cuffs on in twenty minutes. He bought a simple white shirt, a blue and white striped tie, and a pair of black loafers.

He opened the door to Dr. Ralph Williamson's office and approached the receptionist. The office was a lot older than his in California. Brett had a new office with decorator furniture in the reception room and the reception area in his office was open to the business office and the treatment area. This office had old furniture, the rug showed traffic wear and the only contact with the business office was through a sliding glass window which was shut when he entered.

He had to tap on the window twice before he could get the attention of the woman who was talking on the phone. She lifted a finger into the air, signaling him to wait just a minute. When she finally finished her conversation, she slid the window open and looked up at the man dressed in a blue suit and striped tie carrying a black briefcase. "Can I help you?"

Brett opened the wallet so that the receptionist had a clear view of the contents. "Good afternoon, I'm agent Dillon with the National Transportation Safety Board." He handed her a business card.

The gold badge shining through the plastic got the woman's full attention. She took the card, slipped it under her blotter and replied. "What can I do for you?"

"You may be aware that a patient of yours, Tony Russo was killed in a plane crash. It's my job to collect records which may relate to the investigation."

"Oh that was so terrible, both he and his wife were our patients. I better let you talk to Dr. Williamson."

"That would be fine." Brett replied.

The receptionist scurried off into the inner sanctum. When she returned she said, "I'll show you to Doctor's office. He'll be right in."

Brett only had to wait about five minutes before the dentist came into the office. As Brett suspected, he was an older man in his late sixties. He was probably nearing retirement, which would account for the office falling into disrepair. "Hi, I'm Ralph Williamson, horrible about the crash."

Brett handed the dentist his card. "Frank Dillon."

Dr. Williamson looked casually at it. "Fran told me you need some records."

"Yes, I'm sorry to barge in, but we want to wrap up this investigation. You can either copy them or give me the originals. In either case I'll give you a receipt for your protection."

"Hell, just take the originals. By this time next year I'll be fishing everyday anyway."

"That would be great. By the way do you mind if I also take Mrs. Russo's records? These investigations get pretty involved?"

"Take whatever you need. Good luck."

Dr. Williamson shook Brett's hand and was out the door.

Brett scribbled a receipt on a piece of the dentist's stationary, signed it Frank Dillon, and handed it back to the receptionist. He stuffed the records into the black brief case he was carrying, jumped into the rental car and headed for the airport. With luck he could catch a flight tonight and be back in the San Francisco Bay Area by midnight.

Chapter Twenty

Brett had wanted to look through the dental records he had obtained in Minneapolis; however, he was too far behind with his patients to get to them right away. Again he worked through his lunch and finished up with patients just before six o'clock. By the time he had written up his charts it was seven-thirty. He took an apple from the lounge refrigerator and sat down at his desk with the folders containing the records of Maria and Tony Russo.

He opened Maria's folder first and looked at her intake information. She was born November 18, 1966, making her thirty-four years old. She is five foot ten and weighs a hundred and thirty-seven pounds. She stated that she is very concerned about her teeth and her smile and has her teeth cleaned every six months. Her chief complaint is a lower left molar, which has caused her pain ever since she bit down on a cherry pit by accident three weeks ago. She has no children and lists her husband, Tony Russo, as the person to notify in case of an emergency.

Brett removed the x-rays from the folder, placed them on his lighted view box, and began reading the treatment notes.

The first treatment entry was on October 6, 1999. Dr. Williamson had taken a full mouth set of x-rays and a Panorex wide angle x-ray view of the entire jaws and teeth. He noted that the patient had excellent teeth with no restorations. He further noted that tooth #19 had a fracture, which extends into the root structure. Prognosis listed as: *hopeless*. Treatment needed, listed as: *extraction, implant, crown*.

10/20/99

Three carpules of Lidocaine given for lower left mandibular block and infiltration anesthesia. Tooth #19 sectioned in half. Each section removed with elevators and forceps. Bone graft placed in sockets. Two 3.0 silk sutures placed. Prescription for Vicodin #20 1 every 4-6 hours for pain.

10/27/99

Post-op. Site healing well. Remove sutures. Patient to return in 90 days for placement of implant fixture.

1/25/00

Two carpules of Lidocaine given for lower left mandibular block and infiltration anesthesia. Incision on ridge, lay tissue flap back buccal and lingual. Bone fully healed. Drill 10 mm. Place Straumann 10 x 4.5

mm. implant fixture. Place healing cap. Three 3.0 silk sutures placed.
   2/1/00
Site healing well. Remove sutures. Patient to return in 90 days for abutment and crown placement.
   7/1/00
Patient called. Has moved to Colorado. Wants all implant information sent to Dr. Robert Kramer, 2515 Edgewood Dr., Englewood, Colorado, 80110.

Brett finished reading the chart and understood the situation. Maria had left Minneapolis before she was able to get the final work done to replace her fractured tooth. In order for her to get her implant work finished, the dentist in Colorado needed the brand and size of the fixture that Dr. Williamson had placed.

Brett wrote down the information for Dr. Kramer. His office would have the address where Maria is now living. Brett knew he was finally going to meet Maria Russo.

He had finished the apple an hour ago and now he was starving. He went back to the lounge, scrounged through the cabinets, and found two slices of stale bread, a jar of peanut butter and a package of jelly. He made himself a sandwich and hurried back to his office.

He took a big bite of his gourmet dinner and started through Tony Russo's folder. Tony's intake information stated he was born June 10, 1949, making him fifty years old. He was six foot three and weighed two hundred and five pounds. His chief complaint was extreme pain in an upper right bicuspid. He had no children and listed his wife, Maria Russo, as the person to notify in case of an emergency.

The first treatment entry was on January 16, 2000. Dr. Williamson had taken a full mouth set of x-rays and a wide angle Panorex. He noted that the patient had an abscessed tooth #4. Lidocaine was given and an opening was made through the porcelain crown on the tooth to drain the infection. A temporary filling was placed. Treatment needed was listed as: *Root canal.*

1/23/00

One carpule Lidocaine infiltration anesthesia. #4, File canal 21 mm to #30. Fill canal with Gutta Percha and sealer. Place composite filling in access opening.

That didn't provide any information other than Tony had an emergency which was handled very well by Dr. Williamson.

Brett had forgotten to take Maria's x-rays off the lighted opaque viewer. He removed them from under the clips and slid them back into her folder. He reached into Tony's file and pulled out his x-rays. The Panorex was on top so he slipped it under the clips on the viewer. He had a complete view of the upper and lower jaws. He froze. He spoke out loud. "This can't be right."

Brett's brain was trying to process what he was seeing. He jumped to his feet and ran to the reception desk. Ginger kept a ring with every key needed at the office. He fumbled through the keys until he found the one marked STOREROOM.

The storeroom was where Annie was placing all of the files, which had been inactive for the last seven years. She also was storing the files for people who had moved or passed away.

He unlocked the storeroom and switched on the light. Annie was doing a good job; all the files were in perfect alphabetical order. Brett thumbed through the T's and pulled out a file from the deceased section labeled, John Thomas Talbot. He tucked it under his arm, locked the storeroom and hustled back to his office.

When he re-entered his office, it was dark except for the eerie glow of white light coming from the x-ray viewer. Brett reached into J.T.'s chart, picked out his Panorex x-ray, and placed it on the viewer right next to Tony's. He stared at the adjacent films in disbelief. Both of them displayed a small plate with two screws in the right condyle of the mandible.

Not many patients have ever broken their jaw, and of those who have, very few have had a plate placed to set the break. The chance of these two patients having the same break would be one in ten million. Brett pulled out the full mouth x-rays for both J.T. and Tony and began to examine each tooth separately. One by one Brett compared every tooth on the two sets of films; they matched perfectly. There was no doubt that J.T. Talbot and Tony Russo were the same person.

Part III

Clarity

Chapter Twenty-One

It was eleven p.m. and Brett was both physically and mentally fatigued. He had worked on patients for ten hours straight and had spent the last five hours at his desk. Trying to sort out the ramifications of his discovery would have to wait a few hours. He locked up the office and drove back to his townhouse.

As he entered from the garage, Brett could hear his answer machine beeping. He pushed PLAY and Annie's voice came alive. "Brett, I've hardly been able to talk to you since we got home from Italy. Call me, when you get home. I'll be up till midnight."

Brett dialed Annie's number. "Hi, Annie, it's me."

"Oh hi, I didn't think you were going to call. It's almost midnight."

Brett looked at his watch. "Gosh, I'm sorry, I didn't realize what time it was."

"No, it's okay, I just thought you'd be asleep by now."

Brett laughed. "I wish. Just got home from the office. There was tons of paperwork."

"Are you kidding me? You got there at seven this morning. Sixteen hours is too long."

"Thanks for looking after me, but there were some things I had to get settled."

Annie was feeling a little foolish telling Brett how long he should be working. "I didn't mean to sound like a mother again. I'm just concerned you're burning the candle at both ends. It might catch up with you."

"I'm not angry with you. I think I told you I like having someone look after me. I'll take your advice and jump right into bed. Are you working tomorrow?

"Maybe for a couple hours. My project is just about finished."

"I'll see you tomorrow then?"

"Yes, tomorrow. Bye."

Brett showered and got into bed; however, his brain would not relax. He replayed his discovery over and over again in his mind. Finally, at one a.m. he got out of bed and went downstairs to pour himself a brandy.

He settled into the couch and took a sip from the bulbous crystal glass. What should he conclude? J.T. had all the personal information of his former client Tony Russo. Tony had left the country permanently making it an easy task to steal his identity.

Annie told him that J.T. had been gone for two weeks every month over the last couple years. It appeared to Brett that it wasn't for business. Apparently for two weeks each month he was J.T. Talbot living with his wife Annie in California, and for two weeks a month he was Tony Russo living with his wife Maria in Minnesota.

Brett almost felt sorry for J.T.: two wives, two big houses, big debts, and no money.

The peanut butter and jelly sandwich hadn't been much of a dinner and all of a sudden Brett was famished. He went into the kitchen and scrambled up a couple eggs, went back to the living room and washed them down with the Courvoisier from his brandy glass.

As shocking as the information was, there was no doubt J.T. had been leading a double life. He obviously cared for both women; he provided large life insurance policies for each of them and after his death they were well taken care of.

As betrayed as he felt, Brett knew if Annie ever found out the truth, she would be totally devastated. He couldn't bring himself to tell her what he had discovered. He would have to walk a tightrope. He was going to have to find out if J.T. was murdered and find out who died with him in that plane crash, while keeping the other dark secret from Annie.

Brett heard the clock chime three times and he knew he had to get ready for work by six-thirty. He didn't bother to go upstairs; he just turned off the lamp and fell asleep on the couch.

Chapter Twenty-two

Brett made it to the office on time and looked at his daily patient schedule. He was relieved to see that a long appointment from ten-thirty to noon had been cancelled, and he told Ginger not to fill it.

Brett dialed the familiar number for Claude Jennings. "Jennings."

"Claude, its Brett Raven."

"Goddamn it Raven, I told you not to call me again."

"I know, I know, but this is important."

Brett could hear the irritation in the tone of Claude's voice. "You're like a bad case of Jock Rash. Just when I think it's gone, it starts to itch again. I'll talk to you once more and that's it."

"See ya in twenty minutes."

Brett didn't even bother to knock. As usual, Claude was sitting behind the decrepit desk, this time with his feet on top of it. He was leaning back with his hands clamped together behind his chubby neck. He motioned to the dusty chair, which appeared to be reserved for his special guests. Brett snapped his handkerchief over the top of the seat causing the dust to puff into the air.

Claude gave a belly laugh. "Sorry, the cleaning lady was sick this morning. So, what bullshit do you have for me today?"

Brett sat down and threw the two sets of x-rays on the top of the desk next to Claude's feet.

Claude took his feet off the desk. "What the fuck are these?"

"They're x-rays."

Claude snarled. "I look like an orthopedic surgeon to you?"

"They're not orthopedic they're dental."

Claude knew Brett hated smoking. He reached into his bottom drawer where he kept a box of cheap cigars. They were so stale he knew they would smell particularly strong. Again he said, "Mind if I smoke?"

"What difference does it make? You're going to whether I mind or not."

Claude lit the smelly black cylinder. "You know, Raven, I don't like you. As a matter of fact I disliked you the minute you walked into my office a couple months ago."

"That really upsets me, Claude. I was hoping we could go to a couple ball games together."

Claude gave snort. "So why do I want to see

dental x-rays?"

"Because they prove that J.T. and Tony were actually the same person. You told me you met Tony for the first time down in Baja when he was with J.T."

As usual Claude blew a puff of smoke in Brett's direction. "Did I say that?"

"Yeah Claude, you did."

Claude felt in control of the conversation. "I guess I was mistaken."

Brett thought he might use the nice guy disguise. "Claude, I'm not out to get you, I just want to know, what happened to J.T. and why. Can you tell me who was actually in that plane with J.T?"

Claude wasn't buying. "I could, but I won't."

Brett dropped the nice guy routine. "Let me tell you what I think happened in Baja."

Claude responded in a sarcastic tone. "I'm anxious to hear this. You're such a smart guy, I'm sure you have it all figured out."

Brett got up from the chair and looked around. "You have a bottle of water handy?"

"Yeah, I got one." He didn't move.

"Can I have it?"

"No."

Brett stared at Claude and settled back in the chair. "Okay, here's what I think went down. J.T. and our mystery man flew the Baron down to Cabo and you followed in your 206. You brokered a deal to buy organs which were frozen and packed in large crates of dry ice. You cut J.T. in on the deal, and he took a couple crates of the merchandise in his plane and you took a couple crates in your plane. The Rivera brothers didn't want another partner, especially an amateur like J.T. The esteemed police chief managed to get a specialist to change the electronics in J.T.'s S-Tec 60-2 and do a little re-wiring. The fire in the airplane destroyed the evidence, so nobody suspected what the cargo was they were carrying. I'd like to think that you didn't know what was in store for J.T. and his buddy, but I'm not sure."

Claude just sat silently puffing on his cigar. Eventually he spoke. "You think you're so clever. Actually you're a dumb shit. You got it all wrong. The Rivera's deal strictly in cash and J.T. only had $10,000 with him. That doesn't buy much in my type of business."

Brett was nonplussed. Claude sat with a smirk on his face. Finally Brett broke the silence. "Was the $10,000 a down payment? I'm guessing he promised to pay you the balance after the organs were sold."

"Come on Raven, you're the smart guy. Why're you asking me? You figure it out. You decided to stick your nose in here and I'd like nothing better than to see you get it cut off. I suggest you forget about it. I'm sorry your friend and his buddy got killed, but they ain't coming back and if I had anything to do with their deaths, I wouldn't be talking to you right now. Why don't you go back to your dental office, where all the cute little nurses with their big tits think you're a hero, and let this thing die?"

Brett recovered his composure and got up to leave. "I'll call you if I get Giants tickets. We'll have some fun."

Chapter Twenty-three

As usual Brett bumped into Annie during a coffee break. "Hey Annie, what are you doing tonight?"

"Same as last night, nothing. Why?"

"Well I make it a policy to never date an employee, but I'm thinking of making an exception."

"Are you asking me for advice or a date?"

"I value your advice, but this time I'm asking for a date. That new Spielberg movie, 'Saving Private Ryan', is in Palo Alto. Interested?"

Annie looked a bit relieved. "Sure, what time?"

"Starts at eight. Pick you up about seven fifteen?"

"Great."

After the movie Brett and Annie walked down University Avenue to Starbucks. Brett ordered a mocha with extra chocolate and Annie got a vanilla latte.

They talked about the movie for a few minutes until Brett changed the direction of the conversation. "You want to talk about Italy?"

Annie looked down at her latte. "I've been thinking about it a lot. That night meant much more to me than just sex. I've wanted to talk to you about the divorce, but until Italy the opportunity was never there. It was important to me to let you know how I felt.

Brett fiddled around with the packet of sugar next to his coffee until the crystals began to spill on the table. "It was important to me too. You can't believe the weight that was lifted from my shoulders when I was able to admit to you how selfish I had been." He wiped the sugar into a napkin, then purposely spilled it back on the table and nervously began spreading the white flecks around with his finger. "Do you think there's any chance we could start over again?"

Annie was quiet for a moment. "I don't think anyone can start over, but maybe we could pick up where we left off and try to make it better. You know Brett; there were some basic problems with our relationship."

Brett felt a twinge in his stomach. "I realize that now. I made all your decisions for you, didn't I?"

"It wasn't just you. I let you do it. I was young, naïve, and had no confidence in myself.

"Annie, I'm so sorry, I didn't know any better. That's the way I was raised. I always thought that was what a man was supposed to do."

She took his hand. "I'm not really blaming you. I just want you to know if we rekindle our relationship, it has to be different."

He squeezed her hand and pushed away from the table. "I'm going to change. I don't want to hurt you again. If I fall back into my past behavior, kick me in the ass. Hard!"

She smiled. "I'll get my pointed toed boots out of the closet."

Brett drove Annie back to her house and left the engine running as he walked her to the door. He kissed her goodnight and said again, "I'm going to try really hard."

She kissed him back, "Goodnight, Brett."

He drove out of the driveway and down the road that led away from her house. The residents didn't like the appearance of streetlights on their exclusive road, so the only lighting came from the property owners personal lighting systems.

Brett began braking for the stop sign ahead. The only lights on the street were from a front porch, his headlights, and those of a pickup truck a hundred yards behind. As he stopped at the sign he glanced into his rear view mirror, and to his horror, he saw the lights of the truck accelerating toward him.

"Dr. Raven, Dr. Raven, are you awake?"
Brett opened his eyes to see the duty nurse

standing over him and gently shaking his arm. "Yes, I was just dozing."

"You have a visitor, if you're up to talking."

He tried to move his head in the direction of the door, but his neck was too sore to accommodate. "Sure, who is it?'

"Annie. She says she's a good friend."

Brett raised his voice. "Annie, is that you in the doorway?"

Annie came to the bedside and touched Brett's arm. "You don't look too good. Was it the mocha?"

He tried to laugh, but his ribs wouldn't let him.

She realized she had made a mistake. "Sorry, they told me about the ribs."

"Its okay, I'm glad you're here."

Annie's smile disappeared. "Brett, what's going on? Why did those guys beat you up?"

"What guys?"

"The ones who dumped you in my driveway. I was the one who called the ambulance."

He didn't respond to the question. Instead he asked, "How long have you been here?"

"I don't know about twelve hours."

"Annie, I'm fine, I want you to go home and get some sleep. When you come back tonight, there are some things I have to tell you."

"But."

"Please, Annie, I'll explain later."

She leaned over and kissed him on the cheek. "Are you sure you're okay?"

"I'm going to be fine; thanks for being here for

me. Now get some sleep, we'll talk later."

Brett knew he had to tell Annie about J.T.'s illegal activities; however, he couldn't bring himself to tell her about Tony Russo.

Annie returned just before dinnertime. "How're you feeling?"

"Not bad, my ribs are worse than my hand. I guess I'll get a little vacation from dentistry."

"She frowned. "Okay, Brett, let's have it."

"Annie, I've agonized over telling you this, but after our conversation the other night I realize you deserve to know what's going on."

Annie didn't say a word.

Brett continued. "Annie both you and I know that J.T.'s biggest fear was being poor again."

"Yes, I knew that."

"After J.T. lost two million dollars, he was more than poor. He was destitute. He had no money. He had horrendous debts and he had no way to avoid total bankruptcy. A financial counselor who goes bankrupt can kiss all his clients goodbye; J.T. would do anything to avoid that consequence."

"Brett, what are you trying to tell me?"

"Annie, J.T. found out one of his clients was making huge amounts of money on the black market by flying human organs for transplants from Baja to the U.S. J.T. threatened to expose him unless he brought J.T. into a couple deals. He probably figured he could make two or three million dollars in a short period of time."

All of sudden the reality of the scenario hit

Annie. "Brett, the plane crash wasn't an accident was it?"

"No, it wasn't."

Annie's eyes got wide and her breathing became rapid. "Oh, my God," she uttered between deep breaths as she shuffled back onto a chair.

Brett waited until she calmed herself down. "Are you okay?" He asked.

"I'm fine; let me hear the rest of it."

He continued. "I suspected J.T. was involved in the black market deal. That's the reason I went to Mexico."

Annie was starting to get the picture. "That black eye you came back with. You got beat up down there, didn't you?"

"Yeah, apparently I got too close to the truth. This hospital bed is my second warning."

Annie was doing a good job of holding back tears. "That was typical of our marriage. J.T. couldn't even tell me what was bothering him or how desperate he was. I guess I really never knew him." She said, as she dabbed a Kleenex to her eye. "Brett, let it go. You don't owe J.T. anything, and getting yourself killed won't bring him back. Let it go, please."

Brett tried to reach for Annie's hand, but the cast and the IV stopped him. "I will, but I have to make sure I have some insurance against another attack by those thugs. Do you remember the attorney who drew up our wills and trusts?"

"Yes, I remember."

"I want him to come to the hospital; I need him right away. Also, I'm going to take one more trip. Please don't ask me why or where. If I tell you, it will only bring you into this mess. It's safer if you don't know. Hopefully, when I get back the nightmare will be over."

Annie tried to protest.

"Trust me. You just have to trust me." Brett said.

Annie had herself under control. "Please don't let anything happen to you. I don't know what I'd do if it did."

Annie, I promise you, nothing is going to happen to me. Have the attorney come by tomorrow, and by the way, have Ginger drop by."

Annie forced a smile. "She'll be happy. She's called me three times asking, when she can come."

A tray arrived with the nauseating aroma of hospital food. Annie gave Brett another kiss and said, "I'll see you in the morning after I call Ginger and the lawyer." She waved a weak goodbye as she walked from the room.

The nurses changed shifts at six a.m. The day shift nurse entered Brett's room and said, "Good morning, Dr. Raven, how are we doing this morning?"

"I'm not sure how you're doing, but I'm a little sore."

The nurse laughed. "I'm going to bring you an Oxycontin. It will make you feel better."

"I'm going to pass on the narcotics. How about

800 milligrams of Ibuprofen?"

"That's not going to do much. Are you sure?"

"I have a couple important meetings this morning. I have to be clear."

The nurse shrugged. "You're the boss."

At exactly nine a.m. Ginger walked into Brett's room. "I guess the trouble we talked about caught up with you."

"Hi Ginger, I guess it did."

"Are you doing all right?"

"Actually, I am."

Ginger took on her mothering pose. "Brett, you're obviously in danger. You have to go to the police."

"Ginger, you know I appreciate your concern, but I'll be out of this mess soon. Meanwhile, I'm going to need your trust."

"Here we go again. Do you think you're immortal? What now?"

"I'll let you know."

Annie must have been very persuasive. The attorney showed up just after lunch. Brett asked him to close the door and then he began telling him why he was summoned. "I have information regarding criminal activities taking place between a guy in San Mateo and two men in Mexico. I know exactly what's happening, but I don't have enough evidence to prove it. I'm going to get that evidence in a couple weeks, and once I have it, I want it placed in a safe deposit box. I don't want to know where the box is, but I'll pay the annual fee and your annual fee to tend to it. If I am ever beaten up, or left a vegetable, or if I die a violent death, I want you to turn the evidence over to the FBI."

The attorney didn't expect this. "Brett, certainly I'll do what you request, but have you thought this through?"

"Believe me; I've thought it through a hundred times."

"What, if something happens before you get the evidence?"

"I'm just going to have to take the chance, it doesn't. I'll see you at your office in a couple weeks"

Annie and Ginger came in together around two o'clock. Annie touched Brett's good hand. "How you doing?"

"I'm doing great. The doc says I may get out the day after tomorrow."

Annie said, "I'll make chicken soup."

Brett made a face. "Ugh, you know I hate chicken soup. I'm glad both of you are here, I need your help. You know that new dentist, John Gruber, who opened a practice in town six months ago?"

They both nodded.

"I know he can't make ends meet. I want you to ask him if he'll come into my office and cover the practice three days a week. We'll pay him forty percent of all the fees he generates. That will keep the practice going. I have plenty of disability insurance that J.T. sold me, so I'm fine with personal income."

Both women assured him they would get on it that afternoon.

Chapter Twenty-four

Brett's hope of getting out of the hospital in two or three days was unrealistic. His thumb wasn't bothering him, since the plaster cast had immobilized it, but his ribs and neck were so sore he wasn't even able to get out of his bed for the first three days. On the fourth day he was walking up and down the halls, and by the sixth day he was stopping at the nurse's station telling jokes. A week after he was admitted, he was finally ready to go home.

Annie answered the phone. "Hi Annie, guess what? I'm getting sprung this morning."

"Oh, that's great. Do you need me to pick you up?"

"Do you think you could? I hear my car isn't in very good shape."

"Sure, it's ten after ten right now, how about noon?"

"See you then."

The hospital policy required Brett to be taken to the exit in a wheel chair and Annie was there waiting. As Annie helped him out of the chair, she couldn't help but assess his physical appearance. His face looked thin from the weight he had lost during the last week. His usually tan skin had taken on a pale color and with his ribs taped and a neck collar on, he moved very slowly.

Brett was able to navigate into the passenger seat and Annie went around and jumped behind the wheel. "I hear there's a new roller coaster at Great America. Should we stop there on the way to your place?"

Brett shot her a smirk. "I wish."

Annie pulled the SUV into Brett's driveway and ran around to help him out. "It's okay, I can handle it myself."

Brett slid off the seat and managed to get himself started toward the door. Annie wasn't sure what to do. Brett sensed it. "Come on in for a few minutes."

"Okay."

Brett was carrying a little plastic bag with a draw string where the hospital had put all of his personal belongings. He scraped along the bottom and came up with his keys. He opened the door and went in; however, Annie hesitated. "Annie, it's okay, you'll be fine."

Brett started up the stairs slowly. "Make yourself comfortable, I'll be down as soon as I change out of these smelly clothes."

Annie felt a wave of nostalgic longing for all she had left behind five years ago. Every one of the furnishings she and Brett had bought for the townhouse was still there. He had changed nothing. Even their wedding picture was still in its gold frame on the top of the buffet. Next to it was a picture taken in Baja of Annie, Brett and J.T. leaning on the Baron.

Brett didn't give Annie too much time to get lost in the past. He hobbled down the stairs, holding onto the railing. "How 'bout a coke?"

Annie broke out of her daydream. "I'll get them. Sit down."

Annie set the cans on the coffee table and they both sat down on the couch. Brett was the first to speak. "I'm going to need a car. Could you run me down to Hertz?"

"Not today, you're in no shape to drive."

He didn't feel like putting up any resistance. "How about tomorrow morning?"

"Do you think you're really ready?"

Brett emptied his coke. "I have to get to the office and talk to John Gruber. He did say he'd like to cover the practice, right?"

"He's ecstatic. He only has about one or two patients a day in his own office. This may save him from bankruptcy."

"I'll make you a deal. I'll rest all day today if you'll take me to Hertz tomorrow, and if you'll arrange for John to come by the office, so we can tie up the loose ends."

Annie was relieved that Brett would get at least one more day of rest. "I'll come by at ten."

Annie got up to leave. Brett started to get up. "Sit, I'll see you tomorrow." She ran her hand over his cheek and headed for the door.

Chapter Twenty-five

Brett was feeling much better when he got out of bed the next morning. His ribs were not quite as sore and his neck had improved enough for him to abandon the collar. He shaved and showered, put on a clean pair of jeans with a sport shirt, and slipped into a pair of loafers without socks.

As usual, Annie was right on time. "Man, you're looking a hell of lot better than yesterday."

"Thanks, I feel better. Let's get me a car."

Annie dropped Brett off at the rental dealer in San Mateo. "You okay on your own?"

"Absolutely, I have a few errands to run. What time is Gruber coming by the office?"

"I told him about two o'clock."

"Perfect, make sure you and Ginger are there. I want everybody in the loop."

"Okay, I'll tell Ginger. See you at two."

Brett signed out a Chevy Malibu and took it on

a monthly rental. He headed straight for the shop where his Porsche had been towed after the accident.

A big guy with a red beard and the name Rusty printed on his shirt was apparently the owner of the shop. "You sure you want to see it? It ain't a pretty sight."

"I want to."

Rusty led Brett through the shop, where body work was taking place on a half dozen vehicles. He opened the back door that led to a yard filled with cars which had all been reduced to junk. Rusty pointed to the corner of the yard.

As Brett slowly approached the car, he barely recognized his trusty little 356. The Porsche looked about three feet shorter than before. Apparently, the pickup truck used to ram him had an oversized bumper. The Porsche was designed with the engine in the rear and the bumper of the truck had caught the engine door half way up, driving the engine straight into the passenger compartment of the car. When Brett looked through the driver's window, he could see the little four cylinder motor about an inch from the back of his seat. Oil had dripped out and had made a black stream down the leather and onto the front carpet.

Brett knew it was hopeless. The insurance company was going to "total" the car. It would take twice as much to repair than for what it was insured.

He turned to Rusty, who was standing to the rear, with his hands clasped together like a mortician at a casket viewing. "Any chance you could pry that insignia off? I'd like it as a memento."

"Sure." Rusty grabbed a hammer and a screwdriver. He put the screwdriver under the edge of the insignia and tapped it hard with the hammer. It popped off, and he handed it to Brett, who put the little treasure in his pocket. He kissed his hand and touched the hood of the vehicle, then turned away and walked back toward the shop.

When Brett came into his office all the women who worked for him gathered around and told him how good he looked. He knew they were lying, but thanked them all anyway.

John Gruber was waiting in Brett's private office when Ginger, Annie and Brett walked in. He jumped to his feet. "I'm sorry to hear about your auto accident. How're you doing?"

"Thanks John, I'm doing well, but as you can see I won't be drilling teeth for awhile."

"That's what Ginger and Annie told me. Brett, I'm flattered you trust me with your patients. I'll stay on as long as you need me."

Brett stuck out his right hand. "Thanks, John, I'll feel good with them in your care. Ginger will probably be here for her usual twelve hours a day. She'll be your quarterback. I'll hang around as much as I can to introduce you to the patients and make sure they're comfortable. Does the financial agreement work for you?"

"It's very generous, thanks."

They shook hands again and Ginger took Dr. Gruber around the office to get him acquainted with the staff and the equipment.

Annie got up to leave. "Annie thanks for looking after me. I'm going to just lie around and rest for the next few days. I'll check in with you."

Annie touched his good hand and walked out of the office.

CHAPTER TWENTY-SIX

Brett was quite certain he knew what happened to J.T. and he was completely certain what Claude and the Rivera brothers were up to. They had beaten him up as a warning to stay away, but he couldn't be sure they might change their mind and decide to get rid of him once and for all.

Lying in a hospital bed for almost a week had given him time to formulate a plan. In order to save his life he would have to risk it. He needed to get more evidence on the Riveras that could be used as ammunition to back them off.

About a year and half ago at nine-thirty on a Saturday night, Brett had received an emergency dental call. A man, who identified himself as Enrique Guittierez told him his twelve year old son had been hit by a swinging glass door at the mall and his two front teeth were very loose. Brett instructed Mr. Gutierrez to bring his son to the office immediately.

When Brett examined the teeth, they looked even worse than he expected. Both upper front central incisors were dangling by a thread of tissue. He anesthetized the area and asked Mr. Gutierrez for his help retracting his son's upper lip so he could work.

When the area was numb, Brett irrigated and suctioned the clotted blood from the sockets which previously housed the roots of the teeth. He forced the two teeth back into their normal positions and held them in place for five minutes. He dried the damaged teeth and the four other upper front ones. He followed by applying a mild acid to etch the enamel and then bonded a strip of composite, a cosmetic filling material, across the front of all six teeth to splint them together.

"See if you can move 'em." Brett said to the father.

He looked concerned. "I'm afraid to."

"Go ahead, its okay."

Mr. Gutierrez pushed against the teeth. They were solid as a rock. "Doc, that's fantastic!"

Brett walked them to the door and handed the father a prescription for a pain killer. "We're not done with these teeth. I want to look at them in six weeks. When I take the splint off, if the teeth are tight, I'll continue with treatment. If they're loose, they'll need to be extracted."

"Thanks Doc; by the way call me Enrique."

Six weeks later Brett removed the splint and the teeth were tight. Because the blood and nerve supply to the teeth had been severed, he had to perform root canals on them. He finished off the job by bleaching the now dark colored teeth back to their natural color.

As Brett was releasing his patient, Enrique called him aside. "Doc, your receptionist told me the charges total about twenty-eight hundred." He reached into his pocket, pulled out a wad of hundred dollar bills, and counted out thirty of them. "This should cover it. Doc, my business works strictly in cash. I don't want any receipt with my name on it, and as far as I'm concerned, ya' can pocket the money."

Brett had earlier picked up clues from Enrique indicating he didn't want anyone to know his business; it apparently was not looked upon favorably by law enforcement. Brett took the cash and put it in a drawer. "Thanks, Enrique, I'm going to report it as income, but I don't have to say exactly from which patient it came."

"I appreciate it, doc, and thanks again for all your help with my boy. I owe ya one. If I can ever repay the favor, give me a ring."

Only eighteen months had passed since treatment, and the Gutierrez chart was still in the active files. Brett jotted down the cell number for Enrique, went into his private office and dialed it up.

A familiar voice answered. "Enrique here."

"Enrique, this is Brett Raven, I patched up your son's teeth a while back?"

Brett could hear the smile in his voice. "Doc, how ya doin'." I was just saying to my wife the other day, how nice our boy's teeth look. What brings the call?"

"I remembered, when you left my office, you mentioned, if I ever needed a favor to give you a call. Well, I need one. Any chance I could buy you a drink and discuss it?"

"Absolutely, I own a little bar near the tracks in Redwood City. Come on down after work." He gave Brett the address.

"Thanks, Enrique, I'll be there about six."

"By the way doc, the neighborhood is a little rough. If ya have any problems just mention my name; they know me around here. I guarantee you'll be fine."

Brett drove to the address that Enrique had given him; a little rough was an understatement. The bar was the best looking establishment on the street. Most of the stores were boarded up except for a mini market, a liquor store, and a cigarette shop.

He parked his car directly in front of the bar with the thought it may not be there when he returned. He opened the doors to the bar and walked in. There were three guys sitting on stools at the bar drinking beer out of bottles, a couple guys in leather jackets were standing around watching the room, and a huge guy with a bulge under his jacket was tending the door.

"Somethin' I can do for ya?" The doorman asked.

"Enrique Gutierrez is expecting me."

The big man looked to the back of the room where Brett could make out Enrique sitting in a booth. Enrique gave the big man a nod and motioned Brett toward the booth.

"Doc, doc, good to see ya; welcome to my office. Can I get you somethin' to drink?"

Brett slipped into the booth across from Enrique. "Sure a beer would be fine."

Enrique raised two fingers toward the bartender and asked Brett, "So, what can I help ya with?"

"I owned an airplane with another guy until last March when he crashed it in Baja and was killed."

Enrique interrupted. "I remember reading about it. I had no idea it was your partner, sorry."

Brett continued. "Thanks, appreciate it. I had the feeling that the crash was not an accident so I went down to Baja to take a look. I nosed in a little too far and got the shit beat out of me."

Enrique already had it figured out. "So you're going back down."

Brett's drink had arrived and he took a big gulp from the beer. "Yeah, I am. I'm flying down on Friday and I need some muscle to watch my back. It wouldn't hurt, if he could speak Spanish and had a little skill with picking locks."

Enrique was flattered that Brett had asked him. "Pick any one of those guys; they all have the talents you're looking for."

Brett surveyed the six men in the room. One of the guys at the bar didn't seem to fit in with the others. He didn't look tough and had a warm smile on his baby face. "How about the good looking guy with the big smile?"

Enrique looked toward the bar. "Manuel, come on over here." As he approached, Enrique motioned permission for him to sit down.

"Manny, this is Brett. He's a friend of mine. I want you to go down to Baja with him this Friday and make sure he makes it back safe and sound."

Manny shook Brett's hand and said to Enrique, "I promise you he'll make it back in one piece."

Brett took Manny's cell number and got up to leave. "Enrique, I really appreciate this. I want to make sure I can pay either you or Manuel."

Enrique slid out of the booth and slapped Brett on the back. "That won't be necessary. I appreciate everything ya did for my boy. I owe ya a favor. This one's on me!"

Chapter Twenty-seven

Brett had two days to prepare for the trip to Baja. He went back to Peninsula Aviation where he was greeted by the same cute receptionist who had helped him rent the Cessna 182RG. "Hi, remember me? I rented the RG about six weeks ago for a trip to Baja."

The young lady smiled. "Yes, I do. Dr. Raven, right?"

"Good memory. I'm going back to Baja this Friday. Is the RG available?"

The receptionist took out a notebook and looked at the rental calendar. "Oh, I'm sorry, it's gone for two weeks."

Brett's shoulders slumped. "Is there any other plane you would let go to Baja?"

"We have a B55 Baron, but it's a twin."

With two engines the Baron was faster than the Cessna, but used twice as much fuel. "That will work,

I've got about seven hundred hours in Barons."

"You'll still need a new check out with our chief pilot."

"That's no problem. I want to make sure I can fly it with this cast on my thumb anyway."

Brett's experience in his Baron 58 allowed him to easily fly the smaller B55 and the chief pilot was certain the cast would not be a problem. Except for his thumb, all of Brett's fingers had total movement, and he was signed off to rent the plane.

The next stop on Brett's list was Fry's Electronics in San Jose. He had never been in the store and was astounded by its incredible size and enormous inventory. A young man in a white shirt and a skinny black tie approached him. "How can I help you?"

"I need one of those new digital cameras. It has to be small and have a flash."

The clerk took out a pocket size silver model. "Canon just brought this out; it's called their S10."

Brett turned it over in his hand. "How do I use it?"

The clerk smiled. "It's auto focus, just point and push this button; the flash will go off if it needs light."

"That's great, I'll take it. I need something else. Is there such a thing as a small digital voice recorder?"

"Oh, yes, let's go to the back of the store and I'll show you."

Brett followed the salesman to the rear of the store. The young man took out a device about the size of a pack of cigarettes. "This is the Olympus V90. It came out last year."

"Hard to use?"

"No, just make sure the batteries are fresh and push RECORD."

Brett put it into his shirt pocket. "Would it pick up conversation if it's in here?"

"I don't know, let's try it."

The salesman snatched two AAA batteries from the drawer and loaded the recorder. He pushed RECORD and slipped it back into Brett's pocket. "So, how do you like the weather outside?"

Brett responded. "It looks pretty nice, but I hear it may rain tomorrow. How much is the recorder?"

"Ninety-nine dollars." The salesman took the unit out of Brett's pocket, turned off RECORD, and pressed the PLAYBACK button. Except for a slight hiss, they clearly heard, "So, how do you like the weather outside?"

Brett smiled. "I'll take both the camera and the recorder."

After stopping at the bank to pick up several twenty and one hundred dollar bills, Brett went by his office. As usual Ginger was at the front desk directing traffic. "Hi, Brett, how are you doing?"

"I'm doing great. I can move all the fingers except for that thumb. How's our new guy doing with the patients?"

"Very well, everyone seems to like him."

Brett sobered. "Hey, can we talk in my private office?"

"Oh, oh, whenever I hear that, I don't like what comes next." She followed him into the back room.

They sat down in their usual chairs and Ginger got in the first words. "Where are you going this time?"

"Back to Baja."

All the blood seemed to drain from her face. "You can't. They'll kill you this time."

"Ginger, listen to me. If I can get just a little more evidence, I can use it to make sure these guys will stay away from me forever. If I don't get it, I'm afraid they really may kill me."

"Oh God, Brett, how did you get yourself into this?"

"Ginger, it is what it is. I'm only telling you about the trip because I need someone to know where I am. I'm not telling Annie; you're the only person who will know I'm gone."

"How long?"

"Not long. I'm leaving early Friday morning. I'll be home by Sunday night."

"What do I do, if you don't come back?"

Brett took a sealed envelope out of his top drawer. "Give it a week. If I'm not back by the following Friday, call the FBI and give this to them."

"I'm really scared."

Brett took her hands in his. "Try not to worry. If it makes you feel better, I'm taking one of Enrique Gutierrez's bodyguards with me."

That seemed to calm her down. "Be careful."

Brett made two phone calls that evening. The first was to the cell number Manny had given him. A voicemail message answered. "I'm busy, leave a message."

"Manny, this is Brett. We're headed out at six a.m. Friday. Bring any tools you'll need to negotiate a locked door, and bring any other equipment you'll need in case we run into trouble. Call me back so I know you got this message."

Brett dialed Annie's number. "Hello, this is Annie."

"Hi, it's me."

"Oh, hi, Ginger said you dropped by the office, but you left before I could say hello."

"Yeah, sorry. I was late for an appointment. How's it going?"

"I'm fine. I had a five million dollar deposit into my bank account today."

"How do you feel about it?"

"I still feel guilty, but I'm not giving it back, and I'm not giving it to you for a jet airplane."

Brett laughed. "Atta a girl, now you have the right idea. Speaking of airplanes, I'm headed to L.A. for a few days to look at a few. There are three for sale down there. Maybe I can replace the 58."

"That's great. I think you need to get back into flying. When will you be home?"

"Probably Sunday. I'll give you a call."

"Good luck. I hope you find nice one. "Talk to you Sunday."

Just as he hung up with Annie, his phone rang. "Brett here."

"Hey, buddy, it's your babysitter."

Brett laughed. "Hey, Manny, you ready to go?"

"You bet; it sounds like a vacation for a guy in my line of work. Where should I meet you?"

"Don't be so sure about the vacation. You know the San Carlos Airport?"

"Yeah."

"Drop your car in front of the Sky Kitchen at five-thirty a.m. I'll pick you up and we'll be off the ground by six. By the way, do you smoke?"

"Yeah, that okay?"

"It's okay. What do you smoke?"

"Marlboros, why?"

"Make sure to bring a few packs with you. "See ya Friday at five-thirty."

Chapter Twenty-Eight

Manny was already waiting in the Sky Kitchen parking lot when Brett pulled in at five-thirty. All he carried with him was a small canvas bag and a jacket; he tossed both in the back seat as he jumped into the front of the car.

Brett had already done his pre-flight inspection of the Baron the night before. He grabbed his leather overnight case, Manny's bag, and six bottles of water from his car as they prepared for departure.

The route was the same one Brett had taken two months earlier. After landing and departing the plane in Mexicali, they were greeted by the uniformed man who had been there on Brett's first visit. Before the charade of inspecting the plane began, Brett dropped a twenty on the guy and he was waved toward the terminal building.

At the first desk they were greeted by a familiar

face. "Señor Raven, welcome back to Baja."

"Good to see you again, Juan. Anything new?"

Juan looked around, signaled Brett to follow him and headed for the restroom. Juan checked all the stalls, and, when he was satisfied they were alone, he spoke. "Señor Raven, there's a price on your head. Every desk has your name and picture. Anyone, who spots you, is supposed to notify the Cabo police chief."

Brett had anticipated that Jorge Rivera would keep an eye out for him. "Juan, how much would it take to keep the guard and the three guys at the desks quiet?"

Juan thought about it. "I'd give everyone about two hundred dollars, but remember, someone may take the money and turn you in anyway to collect a reward at the other end from Chief Rivera."

Brett opened his wallet and peeled off eight one hundred dollar bills. "Take these to the guys and tell them there will be more, when we check out on the way home. If one of them opens his mouth, they'll all lose out on the money."

Juan nodded, took the bills, and walked out of the restroom ahead of Brett. He watched as Juan made the rounds talking to the guys and distributing the money. When all the cash was in the hands of the workers, Brett signaled Manny and they sat down at the first desk. Within ten minutes they were out of the office and airborne to Punta Pescadero.

Brett knew he couldn't fly into San Jose del Cabo; Jorge would have a snitch positioned there looking for him or anyone else on the Rivera shit list. The day before the trip, Brett had called down to Punta Pescadero, reserved a room for two nights, and requested a rental car be brought up from Cabo San Lucas. The clerk assured him the car would be no problem.

Brett didn't want to show his face at too many airports; however, because no fuel was available in Punta Pescadero, he took a chance and refueled at Loreto less than an hour away from the resort. No one seemed to recognize him, but Brett figured there was a fifty-fifty chance the Riveras would know he was coming even before he arrived.

Brett circled the resort and by the time he landed, the jeep was at the runway to pick them up. He parked the Baron close to the gate which led to the hotel and secured it to the blacktop with tie down ropes. Manny was already waiting in the jeep by the time Brett jumped in.

The clerk recognized Brett as they walked in. "Welcome back, I didn't recognize the name on the reservation. We had that car brought up from Cabo. I know it's too hot to let the top down, but they brought you a Mustang Convertible."

Brett chuckled. "I hope it has air conditioning."

"I wouldn't worry about that. It's a brand new 2000 model."

"We may be leaving really early Sunday morning." Brett gave the clerk his American Express and paid in advance for the room and the car. "Can we just leave the car out near the runway?"

"Sure, just leave the keys in the ignition. We'll get it back to the agency."

The clerk pointed out the room. "Dinner starts at seven."

As Brett and Manny walked toward their room, Brett said, "We both better take a nap. It's going to be a long night. I'll fill you in on the plan at dinner."

They each had a queen size bed and were fast asleep within ten minutes. Three hours later, at seven-thirty, Brett woke up and took a shower. By the time he was done, Manny was awake and on the patio smoking a Marlboro.

Brett walked outside. "Better enjoy the view now; we're not going to be here very long. Let's go to dinner, and I'll tell you the plan."

They took a table away from the other guests and each ordered a Carta Blanca. Brett finished half his beer before speaking. "Okay, Manny, here's the deal. We'll leave here around ten and drive down to Cabo San Lucas. I figure we should be there before midnight. We have to get into the coroner's office at the edge of town."

Manny started to laugh hysterically. "We came all the way down here to break into a joint filled with dead bodies? I was hoping we were gonna steal some jewels or some shit like that."

"Sorry to disappoint you, but don't think this is going to be easy. The coroner's brother is the police chief, and there's a good chance he knows we're here."

Manny lit a cigarette. "What the hell are we going to steal out of a morgue?"

"We're not actually going to steal anything. We're going to take pictures of the coroner's records, but if we get caught, we're in deep shit. We'd be better off as jewel thieves."

Dinner arrived and they dug into the fresh dorado fillets. Manny ordered another beer. "Are there any guards at the morgue?"

"I don't think so. The brothers probably know we're in town, but I doubt they think we would have the balls to break into the coroner's office. We'll watch the place for an hour, and, if it looks deserted, you'll use your expertise to get us inside. I'll go through the records and take the photos while you keep a lookout for visitors."

Manny lit another cigarette. "Holy shit, Brett. I thought you were a wimp tooth doc on some kind a midlife adventure. This thing could get us killed."

"I am a wimp tooth doc. That's why I brought you along."

"What happens after we get the pictures?'

"We'll stay overnight in Cabo. Tomorrow, you're going to interview some of the people whose names we get from the files."

"Why me? I look like a shrink?"

"Manny, there are just two of us and only one speaks Spanish."

Manny shrugged, took the last cigarette from

the Marlboro pack and lit it.

Brett picked up the empty box. "Mind if I keep this?"

"You're somethin' else. We could get killed tonight and you're collecting souvenirs."

Brett put the box in his pocket. "It's nine-thirty. Let's get ready to go."

They stopped off at their room before heading down to Cabo. Brett checked his overnight case to make sure he had the camera, digital recorder, and two high powered flashlights he had packed. Because the plan was to stay overnight in town, they each took their travel cases with them as they headed for the Mustang.

Brett handed the keys to Manny. "I did the flying, you can do the driving." Manny took possession of the left seat.

The town of Cabo San Lucas is seventy miles by car from Punta Pescadero. After leaving the hotel, they had to navigate a narrow rough road for about a mile until they reached the main two lane paved highway. Once on their way they had to pass through a couple small villages and the town of San Jose del Cabo before they drove into the center of Cabo San Lucas.

Brett could tell Manny was an experienced driver by the way he negotiated the Mustang around the potholes and curves of the Baja roads. He had kept his speedometer close to sixty, a good number which wouldn't draw police attention. They arrived at the north end of town at eleven forty-five.

Brett pulled out a street map of the town, along with the napkin on which his bar buddy Carlos had written directions to the coroner's office. "Manny, pull over in that lot just ahead. Let's figure out where we're going."

Together Brett and Manny traced the route they needed. "Let's drive by a couple times without stopping," Manny suggested.

"Good idea."

Manny made two passes by the front of the stone building before he pulled off the road a hundred yards from the coroner's office. The moon was in its waning phase and the night sky was dark except for the stars glimmering overhead.

They peered through the darkness at the building for a half hour. There was no activity around the office, and only one car had passed by during their thirty minute surveillance. Brett picked up the flashlights and the camera. "Bring your tools, let's get this over with."

Manny reached into his bag, brought out a small leather case and put it in his pant's front pocket. As they were getting out of the car, Brett saw him pull a coal black pistol from the case. A chill went up Brett's spine. "Manny, do we really need that?"

"Brett, we better get something straight right now. You brought me along for protection. If we run into trouble, I can't use my bare hands to save us. I'm covering my ass as well as yours, and I'm not going in there without a weapon. It's your choice."

Brett suddenly was bumping up against the reality of the situation that he had created. "You're right. You do your job, and I'll do mine. Just don't use that thing unless you positively have to."

"Don't worry, doc, I won't."

They went around to the back of the building where they were out of sight from the road. Manny examined the back door. "There's a Mickey Mouse alarm on this door. I'll have it disarmed in two minutes."

He opened the leather case and took out a wire and a clipper. He stripped the two wires between the alarm switch and the door. Then he cut off twelve inches from his own wire supply and stripped both ends. When he was sure he had clean wires, he attached one end of his twelve inch piece to the wire that went from the alarm to the door and the other end to the wire that went from the door back to the alarm. After checking for good contacts, he cut the original wires. The system was still in tact, but now it had bypassed the door.

Brett tried the door; it was locked. "Hang on." Manny said. He took a couple small metal instruments from his case and started to tease them into the lock. When he found one that fit, he jiggled it back and forth until he heard a click. The door opened.

They both lit their flashlights as they entered the building. Brett remembered the configuration of the facility and headed down the long hallway which led to Dr. Rivera's office.

Inside the office Brett went straight to the metal file cabinet he had seen on his first visit. "Manny, I need your help, they're locked."

Manny had the drawers opened in thirty seconds. Brett started from the top. "I'm going through these files. Why don't you go outside and keep an eye open."

"Okay, first I'm unlocking the front door. If we have visitors, you get the hell out of here through the opposite door they come in."

Brett felt good having a pro with him. "I get it."

One by one Brett started through the files. When he came to one which indicated organs had been removed from a deceased, he took a digital photo of the file jacket and its contents. After forty-five minutes he had pictures of about twenty folders.

Manny stuck his head in the back door. "Brett, we're pushing our luck if we stay any longer. Finish it up."

Brett closed the cabinet drawers and pushed the locking buttons back in place. He went to the front door to re-lock it and then exited through the back where they had come in.

Manny went to work on the alarm. He reattached the original alarm wires and removed his bypass wire. He took two small pieces of black tape, covered the cuts he had made, and tucked the wires under the molding where they were not readily visible. "Let's get out of here."

Manny pulled the Mustang into the Finisterra parking lot at two a.m. Brett paid cash for a room; they were fast asleep by two-thirty.

By the time Manny woke at eleven o'clock, Brett had already been up for an hour. He was methodically going through the pictures in his digital camera. Alongside him was a large yellow legal tablet on which he was listing names and addresses. "Hey, Manny, sleeping a little late, aren't you?"

"Tough night's work. Does this job come with breakfast?"

Brett looked at his watch. "Yeah, get dressed. We'll go downstairs."

As he ate his huevos rancheros, Brett outlined their next task. "The police chief down here is a municipal cop. He gets trumped by state and federal. You're gonna impersonate a Federale, a federal cop, when you do your interviews this afternoon."

"Why would anyone believe I'm a Federale?"

Brett took out his wallet and handed it to Manny. "Open it up."

Manny opened the wallet and stared at the gleaming gold sheriff badge. "Whoa, where did you get that?"

"Doesn't matter, the point is when you flash it, you'll scare the hell out of the people you're talking to. They won't bother to check where it's from and they'll tell you what you want to know."

Manny closed the wallet and handed it back to Brett. "What do I ask them?"

"You tell them you're investigating Dr. Rivera. Make sure they're a relative of the deceased, and then ask them if they knew organs were removed from their loved one just after he or she died. If they say yes, ask if they were paid. If they say no, ask how they feel finding out about it."

"Brett, I won't be able to remember all these conversations."

Brett pulled out the Marlboro box he had taken from Manny yesterday and pushed it across the table. Manny examined it and saw that an opening had been cut out in the front of the box.

"Open it up," Brett said.

Inside was neatly tucked the digital recorder. The microphone was carefully aligned with the hole in the front of the cigarette box.

"When this is sticking out of your shirt pocket, it will look like an ordinary box of Marlboros."

Manny smiled, "You know doc, if you ever quit the tooth business, I think Enrique could use you."

After breakfast Brett went back to work making a master list to match up the relatives with the deceased. He also had to note addresses and mark them on the street map. By three o'clock he was ready to put his Federale to work.

Brett gave Manny the gold badge which he would use when he introduced himself as a federal cop. He also showed him how to start the recorder before approaching to the door.

He had photographed twenty files, but eight of the addresses were not even on the map. Brett had written down the remaining twelve, and one by one Manny approached each door while Brett sat in the Mustang to keep an eye out for trouble. Six of the twelve addresses hadn't produced the person on Brett's list, so by the end of the day, he obtained just six taped conversations from the twenty folders he had photographed.

It was eight p.m. by the time Brett and Manny had showered and stowed their cases in the Mustang. Both of them were starved. Brett figured they had better eat now because by the time they got back to Punta Pescadero, the kitchen would be closed.

They were finishing their meal when Brett spotted him. At the front desk he caught site of a police uniform and as the man turned toward the dining room he recognized Jorge Rivera. "Manny, we have company. Just get up and follow me to the back door. We gotta get the hell out of here, now."

Brett tossed the keys to Manny and they both jumped into the front seats. As Manny screeched out of the parking lot they caught site of a police car with a driver parked at the front entrance. "Maybe he didn't see us." Manny said.

"We made eye contact. He saw us." Brett said, as he looked through the rear window.

There were no other cars on the road and it was dark by the time Cabo disappeared from the rear view mirror. Manny accelerated to seventy-five and headed north toward Punta Pescadero. Twenty miles out of town Manny glanced again at the mirror. "Oh, oh, bogies at six o'clock."

Brett looked behind them. Two headlights and a flashing red one were closing quickly on them. Manny floored the accelerator. The tires peeled rubber as the Mustang sprang forward and in twenty seconds the speedometer was reading one-o-five.

The lights behind them disappeared, but five minutes later they reappeared and were getting larger. Manny switched off his lights.

It was still thirty miles to Punta Pescadero, and at the speed they were travelling it would take another twenty minutes. Manny glanced at the rear view mirror. Rivera's car was slowly gaining on them. "How long will it take to get the engines started on the plane?"

"If everything works, about five minutes."

"Is the gate we used the only one to the runway?"

"Yeah, that's how they keep it secure."

It was pitch black and Manny was having trouble keeping the Mustang off the shoulder. "I'm gonna put you right at the gate. Start the engines and pull it on the runway. I can hold 'em off for five minutes, and then I'll make a run to the plane and we're out of here." He took the pistol from his pocket and placed it on the console.

Manny knew they were getting close; he slowed down to sixty and turned the headlights back on. The police car saw the lights and closed to within three hundred yards. A sign, BIENVENIDO A PUNTA PESCADERO, was illuminated by the Mustang's headlights. Manny hit the brakes, took a ninety degree right, and floored it down the dirt road to the lodge.

The Mustang skidded to a stop in front of the airport gate. Brett grabbed the two overnight cases, jumped out of the car and headed for the airplane. "Five minutes," Manny yelled.

While Brett was dialing the code to enter the gate, Manny positioned himself between the Mustang and the airport. Brett scurried through the gate, propped it open with a rock, and reached the plane at the same time the police car came racing onto the property.

Brett hurriedly untied the ropes that were securing the Baron to the blacktop, unlocked the plane, and slid into the pilot seat. Normally, he used a check list prior to starting the engines, but today he relied on his memory.

Manny heard the first engine start just as Captain Rivera and his companion officer catapulted out of the police car. Manny took aim and shot the left headlight out. The two policemen dropped to the ground and scrambled under the sides of the vehicle. Manny fired again and shot out the right headlight. Rivera hadn't expected resistance of this sort and both men stayed flat on their stomachs.

Brett got the second engine started and quickly taxied the Baron onto the runway into position for takeoff. Manny fired one more shot which exploded the windshield of the police car, and then he made a dash toward the open gate.

Brett saw Manny running toward the plane and pushed the door wide open. Manny crawled up the wing into the right seat and locked the door shut. "Go, go," he shouted. Brett advanced the throttles full forward and the Baron responded with a roar as it hurdled down the runway. They were airborne fifteen seconds later.

Once the Baron was leveled off at eighty-five hundred feet and set to fly on the autopilot, Brett turned to Manny. They both broke out in laughter and gave each other a high five. "We're going to have to break a few more rules tonight," Brett said.

"What d'ya mean?"

"Number one, it's illegal to fly an airplane in Mexico after sunset unless it's an instrument flight. Number two, there's no way we can stop at Mexicali to check out of Baja. They'll arrest us. Number three, we can't check in with U.S. customs until tomorrow, which means we'll be in the U.S. illegally tonight."

Manny was unfazed. "Does it matter?"

"Only, if we get caught. We'll fly into Imperial, a small uncontrolled airport about fifteen miles north of Calexico. Tomorrow morning we'll call customs and tell them we're in Baja and will be crossing the border in an hour to check in at Calexico. They won't know we're really coming from Imperial."

"Don't they watch the radar?"

"We'll fly at three hundred feet, too low for radar."

By the time they landed at Imperial, it was two forty-five a.m. There was no way to get from the airport into town so Brett and Manny closed the window curtains, reclined the seats in the plane, and dozed off to sleep.

Brett had parked the Baron facing east; by seven-thirty the sun was streaming in through the front windshield. He could hear activity on the airport and he looked over at Manny. "You awake?"

"Yeah, I'm awake."

"How were the accommodations?"

"Believe me, I've had worse."

Brett peeked out through the curtains. "Grab the overnight cases." He said as he opened the front door.

Manny followed Brett out of the front door and they both hopped off the wing onto the blacktop. There was a small terminal building thirty yards away and they headed toward it with their cases in hand.

A young guy in coveralls with the name Rich sewed on his pocket was sitting at the desk. "Hey, where did you guys come from, I didn't see you land."

Manny let Brett do the talking. "Got in a couple hours ago from New Mexico. Can you top off all my tanks?"

"Sure."

"Any way we can get into town and grab some breakfast?"

The young man reached in his pocket. "Take my pickup; it's only about a mile."

"Great, we'll have it back in an hour."

"Take your time, I'm here all day."

They found a Denny's on the main drag and went in with their cases. After recharging with bacon and eggs, Brett poured himself another cup of coffee. "Let's use the restroom to shave and put on clean shirts. I don't want customs to think we're anything other than a couple of tourists."

They arrived back at the terminal at nine-thirty. Brett put the box of Marlboros on the counter and handed the keys to the young guy who had loaned them his truck. "Thanks that was nice of you to let us use it." He opened his wallet and flashed the sheriff badge that had come in handy so many times the last few months. "Rich, can I ask you some questions in confidence?"

Rich glanced down at the badge. "Yes, sir."

"You can't mention to anyone we were here today. We're on a mission being run by the DEA and we think drugs may have been off loaded right here at Imperial Airport."

"You shitting me? Here?"

Brett put his wallet with the badge back to the

safety of his back pocket. "Have you ever seen a Cessna 206 come in here and remove cargo?"

Rich's eyes opened wide and he pointed toward a row of six buildings. "Every month a short fat guy comes in and unloads right over there in hangar number twenty-seven. He pays me twenty bucks to help him lift a couple crates out of the plane and into the hangar; he flies off, comes back two hours later, and pays me twenty bucks to help him reload the cargo back into the plane before he heads out again."

Brett fumbled through his case and found the pictures he had taken of Claude. "Is this the man?"

Rich took the photo. "Yeah, that's him."

"Anything else strange about his behavior?"

"Yeah, the crates are really cold. He gives me special gloves to use."

"Rich, would you write down your full name, address and phone number. We may need to have you testify if we catch this guy."

Rich was beaming. "Absolutely, I'm glad to help." He gave Brett the slip of paper with the information. "Anything else I can do to help, just let me know."

Brett took the Marlboros off the counter and put them back in his shirt pocket. "That's great. Remember, you didn't see us here today, and if that guy shows up, don't worry, we have him under surveillance."

"Yes, sir, I understand."

At ten o'clock Brett got on his radio and called

San Diego Flight Service. "Baron eight, five, Juliet, Sierra is one hour from Calexico requesting customs inspection."

"Thank you five, Juliet, Sierra we'll alert customs in Calexico."

Brett started his engines at ten forty-five, was in the air by eleven, and landed five minutes later in Calexico. He was glad now he had picked Manny from the lineup in the bar. He didn't look tough and with his cleanly shaven face he looked more professional than Brett.

The customs agent wanted to go to lunch and wasn't interested in detaining two American tourists returning from a fishing trip. They were on their way to San Carlos twenty minutes later.

Brett drove Manny back to the parking lot. He walked with him to the car and thrust out his hand. "Manny, I can't thank you enough. You're a pro."

To Brett's surprise, Manny gave him a bear hug. "Doc, ya surprised me. You were as cool as they come. If you ever need help again, I want ya to call me."

Brett gave him a hug back. "Thanks, Manny, I will."

Chapter Twenty-nine

It was four o'clock in the afternoon by the time Brett opened the door to his townhouse. He threw the newspapers on the kitchen table and hit the answering machine. "Hi Brett, welcome home. I hope you found a plane. Give me a call if it's not too late."

Annie answered on the first ring.

"Hi, I'm home." Brett said.

"How was it? Did you find a new plane?"

"No, they sounded better than they looked."

Brett could hear the disappointment in her voice. "Sorry, you need to get back into flying right away."

"Don't worry, I will. How about getting a burger later?"

"Great."

"I'll pick you up at six-thirty."

Brett chose the Oasis, a little dive a few blocks

from the Stanford campus. Annie opened the conversation. "I'll be done with the files in a day or two. I guess I'll have to collect unemployment."

"There's a lot of other stuff that needs attention. Having a substitute dentist has created extra work for the front desk. Do you want to stay on and help?"

"Brett, you succeeded in getting me out of my funk. You don't have to manufacture work to keep me busy."

"Think about it anyway." He changed the subject. "Remember, when I was in the hospital, I told you I had one more trip to make before I can let go of this mess?"

"I was hoping you'd changed your mind."

"I'm leaving early this coming Friday morning."

"I promised I wouldn't pry, so I won't. Just be careful."

"I will. I'll probably see you at the office before I leave. I want to stop by and check in on John."

Brett dropped Annie off and was back home in bed by nine o'clock.

Chapter Thirty

Brett was camped on his attorney, Jim Morgan's, doorstep, when he arrived on Monday morning.

Jim directed Brett into his private office. "I'm guessing you have the evidence you were looking for."

"I've got it all right here." He placed the digital camera and the digital recorder on the desk.

"What do I do with these?'

"The camera contains complete photos of six files from a Mexican coroner's records. I want you to make three copies of all of them. I'll need two copies and you keep one for the safe deposit box."

"What do I do with the recorder?"

"Can you get a hold of a court reporter who speaks Spanish?"

"That's no problem."

"Good, there are seven interviews on the recorder. Have her translate and transcribe each of them. Six will match up with the names on the files. The files are also in Spanish and will need translation and transcription. Have your secretary create a dossier for all six. Include the photos of each file with its transcription along with the matching transcribed interview."

Jim was digesting the information as fast as Brett was hurling it at him. "What about the seventh interview."

"That one's in English already. Just have it transcribed. You keep one copy; I get two."

"Okay, all this stuff will go into the safe deposit box, anything else?"

"Yes, here's an envelope which contains information on a guy named Claude Jennings and information on an operation called The San Francisco Bay Area Transplant Surgical Center. I want it in the box with the dossiers, the memory card of photos, and the digital recorder."

"When do you want the dossiers and the safe deposit box?"

"I need them by Wednesday morning. Remember, I can't know where the safe deposit box is located."

Jim nodded his head. "I understand. By the way Brett, thanks for putting some excitement into the dull life of an estate planning attorney."

Brett laughed. "My pleasure, I'll pick up the dossiers and my camera Wednesday morning."

Brett dialed Claude's number. "Jennings."

"Hello Claude, guess who?"

"You stupid asshole, I told you to mind your business. You even got a gentle warning, but that wasn't enough. You went and made trouble in the enemy's backyard, and now they're gonna kill you for it."

"I don't think so. You have a pencil handy?"

"A what?"

"A pencil, you fat prick, a pencil"

"Yeah, I got one.'

"Okay, take down this address." Brett gave him the directions to Enrique's bar. "You're going to meet me there Wednesday at noon."

"And if I don't?"

"Then you'll either be dead or spending the next twenty years in federal prison."

There was silence on the other end of the phone. "Why the fuck can't you let go of this?"

"Wednesday at noon," Brett said and hung up.

Chapter Thirty-One

Brett arrived at the bar early and briefed Enrique on his upcoming meeting with Claude. Enrique purposely placed his biggest and most menacing bodyguard, Gerardo, at the door.

Claude walked through the door precisely at noon. A large hand pushed against his sternum causing him to lose a breath. "What's your business here?"

Claude's eyes opened as wide as saucers. "I must be in the wrong place. I'm supposed to meet a guy named Raven around here."

"He's in the booth near the back," Gerardo said as he took his hand off Claude's shirt.

Claude walked to the rear of the room intimidated by the three guys watching him from their bar stools. He slid into the booth across from Brett. "What the fuck. Why are we meeting here?"

Brett smiled at Claude. "These guys are my

friends. Since I've already met your friends, I thought it would be nice if you met mine, just in case we start socializing in the future."

Perspiration was forming on Claude's upper lip. "Okay, if I smoke in here?"

"You know its okay with me, I love cigar smoke, but I don't think the owner would like it."

Claude tried to gain his composure. "So, why am I here?"

Brett slid one of the two 11 x 13 envelopes that were lying on the table over to him. "Open it up."

For the first time Brett read genuine fear on Claude's face as he hesitantly removed the documents. "What are these?"

"The six folders on top contain files copied from Miguel Rivera's office. They're all pretty much the same, so we'll just go over the first one."

Brett opened his copy of the file.

"Hector Martinez was killed in a motorcycle accident on February 12, 2000 and was brought to Dr. Rivera's morgue. Turn to the second page and read the third line down. It's been translated into English."

Claude did as he was told. "Removed two kidneys, heart, and pancreas. Flushed with saline and placed in first stage compartment for lowering temperature to minus fifty."

"How, how'd you get these?"

"That's not important. Read the last two lines on the page."

Claude wiped his face with a paper napkin which

he had pulled from the vertical metal container at the end of the table. "Prepare for shipment with C. Jennings. Package deal $50,000 U.S."

Brett skipped to the next page. "Read the interview with Rosa Martinez, Hector's mother."

By now Claude was completely submissive.

"Hello Mrs. Martinez, my name is Manuel Cruz, I'm a federal officer."

"We're just a poor family. We don't do nothing bad."

"I'm sorry, it's not about you. We are investigating Dr. Rivera, the coroner. Did your son Hector die in a motorcycle accident on February 12th?

"Yes, yes he did."

"Was he taken to a hospital?"

"No, they say he was dead. They take him directly to the morgue."

"Did you give permission or get paid to have any of Hector's organs removed?"

"I don't know what you mean."

"Mrs. Martinez, Dr. Rivera removed several of Hector's body parts before he was sent to the funeral home. Did you know that?"

"Oh my God. No, no."

"Would you have given permission for those procedures?'

"No, no."

"I'm sorry I had to tell you about this. Please don't discuss this conversation with anyone, especially Dr. Rivera."

"I understand. Thank you."

"Goodbye, Mrs. Rivera."

"Goodbye."

Brett closed the file and picked up another item in the envelope. "Claude, if you look under the folders, you'll find a transcription of a conversation I had with a gas attendant at Imperial Airport."

Claude located the paper. "Do I have to read it?"

"That's what you're here for, read it."

Claude looked as if he wanted to cry as he started to read. "Have you ever seen a Cessna 206 come in here and remove cargo?"

"Every month a short fat guy comes in and unloads right over there in hangar number twenty-seven. He pays me twenty bucks to help him lift a couple crates out of the plane and into the hangar; then he flies off, comes back two hours later, and pays me twenty bucks to help him reload the cargo back into the plane before he heads out again."

Brett looked Claude straight in the eyes. "That happens to be how long it takes to go back and check into the country at Calexico. I know. I did it."

Claude was white as a sheet. "What else do you have?"

"I talked with Mr. Chris Shaw at the San Francisco Bay Area Surgical Transplant Center. He knows you quite well and stated you are involved in transportation of organs to their facility. You'll find my statement at the bottom of the pile. There's also a financing agreement describing how they fleece sick people out of their homes."

"Are you going to give these documents to anyone?"

"I already did."

Claude jumped out of his seat and started to yell. "You stupid son of a bitch; They'll kill both of us."

All of a sudden Gerardo was at the booth. "Is everything okay, Dr. Raven?"

"Everything's fine, Gerardo. Mr. Jennings is just getting ready to leave."

Brett turned back to Claude. "They're not going to kill anyone. I gave all these documents along with the original photos and recordings to an attorney, who put them in a safe deposit box. I have no idea where the box is, so trying to beat it out of me won't work. If anything happens to me, if I die a violent death, the documents will be turned over to the FBI."

Brett put his set of documents back in the envelope and handed it to Claude. "I want you to give this copy to the Rivera brothers and let them know about the safe deposit box. Who knows, they may even want to give me a bodyguard to protect their interests."

Claude was exhausted. "Can I leave now?"

"Not quite. I'm going to have a $10,000 deductible payment due to the hospital. I'm also going to lose six months of work. I make $12,000 a month. You will deliver a check for $82,000 to my office by this time tomorrow."

"Is that it?"

"No, I want you to deliver another check for $100,000 made out to the United Network for Organ Sharing. I'll make sure they get it.

"Are you kidding me? I can't afford that."

"Why don't you share the expenses with the Rivera brothers? I'm sure they'll think it's a good investment. By the way would you give them a message for me?"

"What?"

"Tell each of them, FUCK YOU from Brett Raven."

CHAPTER THIRTY-TWO

Brett left his townhouse at five on Friday morning. He hoped to be home by early Saturday afternoon, so a small carry-on was all he took with him. Before going to the airport he stopped at his office to check for messages; on his desk was a sealed envelope with a note from Ginger:

> *Some creep dropped this off for you. Be*
> *careful when you open it. It's probably*
> *a bomb.*

Brett laughed as he looked inside and found the two checks from Claude.

His flight took off at six-thirty and landed on time at five minutes after ten Denver time. He went straight to the Hertz counter and picked up a compact Chevy along with a map of the Denver area.

Before pulling out of the parking lot, he reached into his pocket for the address of Dr. Kramer, the dentist, who had requested the implant information for Maria.

2525 Edgewood Dr. Suite 12
Englewood, Colorado, 80110.

Brett located Englewood on his map. As a suburb of Denver it looked to be only about ten miles south of the airport off I-25. The dental office on Edgewood Dr. was another mile and half from the interstate. Brett looked at his watch; it was eleven o'clock, and he wanted to be at Dr. Kramer's office by eleven forty-five.

Brett pulled the Chevy into the medical building complex at eleven forty and located the entrance to Dr. Kramer's office. He parked where he had a good view of the front door, which was for patients, and the side door, which staff would normally use.

At five after twelve two patients left through the front door. At twelve fifteen three women dressed in blue scrubs left through the side door. Finally, at twelve-thirty a nice looking man in his late forties, dressed in slacks and a short sleeved sport shirt, left through the side door. He waited another five minutes, but neither door opened.

Most dental offices take lunch between twelve and one-thirty. Normally one person takes a late lunch, allowing the reception desk to stay open during the break. If Brett had calculated correctly, everyone had gone to lunch except for the one receptionist.

He strolled up to the front door and walked into the reception room. The office was quiet except for the elevator music streaming softly through the ceiling speaker. Brett approached the receptionist who looked up and said, "Hello, may I help you?"

Brett put his left hand with the cast on the counter; his forehead bruise was in full view. "Yes, I was referred to Dr. Kramer. I had an auto accident last week, and I think I may have cracked some teeth."

"Oh, I'm sorry to hear that. The doctor is out to lunch, and he's pretty booked up this afternoon. Are you in pain?"

"No, no, I don't have to be seen today. I'd just like to make an appointment, whenever he has space available."

The receptionist looked relieved. "I'll give you a new patient information form. You can fill it out, and we'll set up an appointment as soon as possible."

"That would be fine." Brett took the form and filled it out with the name he had used in Minneapolis, Frank Dillon. He made up a phony address.

As he filled out the form he studied the business office arrangement. It was a very open atmosphere. Patients could wander from the reception room into a large hallway which led to the restrooms and the treatment rooms. The patient files were in alphabetical order, color-coded, and housed in open cabinets along one side of the wide hall. The section containing the "R's" was about ten feet from the reception desk.

The receptionist took the form and looked into the appointment book. "Would next Friday at eleven be good?"

"That would be fine."

She filled out an appointment card and handed it to Brett. "Is there anything else I can do for you?"

"I hate to ask, but, ever since the accident, I get these bad headaches. Would you by chance have some Aspirin or Motrin handy?"

"Oh sure, I'll go back to the lounge and get some. Which do you prefer?"

"Either one would be fine. I'm sorry to bother you."

"It's no bother," the woman said as she scurried down the hall.

Brett had to move fast. He went straight to section 'R'. He ran his fingers up and down the files until he located 'RUS'. Three files to his right was the one he needed, Maria Russo. He snatched it from the cabinet, placed it on the floor, removed the Canon S10 from his pocket and clicked off three shots of the front of the chart. He replaced the file back into the proper section just as the receptionist turned the corner.

Brett could see he had startled her by being in the hallway. "I was looking for some water."

"Oh, here's the aspirin. The restroom is the second door. You'll find cups on the counter."

Brett thanked her and went into the restroom. He flushed the pills down the toilet and returned to the desk. "Thanks again, I'll see you next Friday" he said as he walked out the door.

Back in the car, he took the camera from his pocket and turned the selector dial to REVIEW. He scrolled the three photos and smiled. Finally he had the Russo address.

He drove up the street to the address he had gotten from the photo. It wasn't a very nice neighborhood. There were no single family homes, only apartments. He noticed a sign that read: **rent one month get the second month free**.

He parked the car and walked into the apartment complex. The unit he was looking for was on the second level and there was no doorbell. He knocked on the door. No one responded. He knocked harder a second time. The door opened. Brett looked the man straight in the eyes and said, "Hello, J.T."

Chapter Thirty-three

J.T. stood frozen. "Aren't you going to ask me in?" Brett said.

He recovered his composure. "Brett, I know you don't believe me, but it's great to see you again. Sure, come in."

Brett looked around the apartment. It was very small, probably only one bedroom. The furniture was generic and he guessed it came with the rental. "This doesn't look like you J.T. Have you fallen on bad times?"

J.T. looked a little embarrassed. "Actually we're only here for three more days. We're moving to a new house on the east coast. Pretty much living out of suitcases right now."

J.T. motioned Brett toward the small living room. Just then a tall attractive woman with blond hair and a beautiful figure came out of the bedroom. "Maria, this is an old friend, Brett

Raven."

All of the blood drained from Maria's face. They knew no one in Colorado, and the appearance of this stranger was a signal of danger. She looked right past Brett and spoke to J.T. "Tony, I'm going out shopping; I'll see you in an hour."

The door slammed behind her. Brett asked J.T. "Does she know?"

"She knows about the insurance scheme, but she doesn't know about either you or Annie."

They sat down on the vinyl couch. "You look pretty good for a guy whose funeral I attended five months ago."

J.T. responded. "You don't look so good. What happened to your head and your wrist?"

"That was a present from your business partners, Claude and the Rivera brothers."

J.T. looked despondent. "Brett, why did you get involved?

"The NTSB accused you of being a negligent pilot, and it looked to me like you had been murdered. For some crazy reason I thought I owed it to you to find out what really happened."

J.T. had a blank look on his face. "I wish I could thank you, but I can't. I'm afraid you opened a can of worms." He became silent as he gave his situation some thought. "It's my guess you went to Minneapolis."

"Yeah, I did"

"You located those x-rays of my jaw, didn't you?"

"Right again."

"I knew the minute Dr. Williamson took them that I had made a mistake. I should have toughed it out and waited to get back to California."

Brett again looked J.T. straight in the eyes. "J.T., tell me why. Make me understand."

J.T. looked down at the floor for at least a minute. "Brett, I screwed up. I counseled my clients not to take big risks, but, when I saw a chance to make a killing, I bet the ranch and I lost. You know my background; I'd rather be dead than poor again."

"I get that. I get it, but, what about Annie? How could you betray her that way?"

Now J.T.'s voice was starting to crack. "Brett, you have to understand. The marriage to Annie was a huge mistake. I was going to ask for a divorce, but, when this deal came up, I figured it wasn't necessary."

Brett smirked. "So instead you became a fucking bigamist."

J.T. ignored the insult. "I started seeing Maria a couple years ago. It was mainly a physical thing, but after I lost the two million, I needed to take Tony's identity and I had to be married for Maria to collect the insurance proceeds. The marriage was actually a business decision. I never wanted to hurt Annie. Hell, I used the last fifty thousand I had in the bank to buy that five mill policy for her. How's she doing? Is she okay?"

"She's doing pretty well. I told her you were

probably involved in something shady, but I didn't say anything about Tony or the fact that I figured out what really happened."

"Thanks."

"I didn't do it for you. I did it for her. Tell me J.T., how did you get the guts to jump out of the Baron after the experience you had skydiving?"

J.T. got up off the couch. "Can I get you a drink? I think I need one."

Brett didn't want any alcohol. "I'll take a Coke."

J.T. went into the kitchen and returned with a beer and a Pepsi. "It was the only way. It had to look like Tony and I died in that plane crash. I'd made two jumps before; I figured lightening wouldn't strike me twice. Actually, I made a perfect landing on both feet instead of my head"

"After my last meeting with Claude, I realized you never were interested in organs. You paid Miguel Rivera $10,000 for those two bodies that burned up in the pilot and co-pilot seats. I just can't figure out how you were able to get them from the crates into the seats."

J.T. took a long slug off the beer. "You're a medical man; you must know that the human body is over fifty percent water. When it dehydrates after death, it gets pretty light. It wasn't a problem at all."

"Okay but how did you know the fire would consume them?"

"Come on Brett, you know I wouldn't have left that to chance. I had a ten gallon can of auto gas. I poured it all over the bodies and the crates in the back of the plane. I strapped on the chute, threw the can out the door, lit the fuel, and did a swan dive out of the plane."

Brett was barely drinking from the Pepsi can. "The uniformed guard in Loreto told me you took off with the side door open. I knew that wasn't like you; it made me very suspicious."

J.T. looked surprised. "You went down to Baja?"

"I did. That's how I found out about the crates and the open door. I also found out that Claude was with you. I was leaving Cabo when I got the shit kicked out of me by Chief Rivera's goons."

"Goddamit, I wish you hadn't got involved in this."

Brett shrugged it off. "Speaking of Claude, you must have had a lot of goods on him to get him to help you."

"I sold Claude a big life insurance policy among other things. Believe it or not he actually has a wife. Can you believe someone would marry that slimy little worm?"

That got the first smile of the day out of Brett.

J.T. continued, "I stumbled on his dealings in Baja. He had to help me or I threatened to expose his black market business."

Brett wanted to squeeze a little more out of J.T. "I know Claude took off from Cabo two hours before you. I figure he flew to San Felipe ahead of you and rented a car. He was probably waiting south of town until he saw the Baron go down. Then he drove another thirty miles to pick you up."

J.T. looked at Brett with admiration. "I knew you were smart, but not that smart. You pretty much have it right. Everything was ready to go a hundred miles before San Felipe. The bodies were strapped in the seats and the plane was flying on the autopilot. When the distance measuring equipment read sixty miles to San Felipe, I switched the autopilot to descend at a rate of five hundred feet per minute. I calculated the Baron would hit the ground in thirty miles. I lit the gas and jumped."

"So all Claude had to do was drive sixty miles south of town and pick you up."

"Exactly, we actually passed the crash on our way back to town."

"I examined the plane when I flew down to Baja. I don't know if I can forgive you for destroying our precious piece of machinery."

J.T. fetched himself another beer. "Come on Brett. You got almost two hundred thousand from the insurance. You can go out and buy an even better one."

"Can't you measure anything without using dollar signs? That plane and its memories meant more to me than an insurance check."

J.T.'s mood became morose. Tears came to his eyes and he began to cry. "Our years flying together were the best years of my life. The guys at the kitchen used to call us the Three Musketeers. I loved that plane too. I loved you guys so much. Brett I'm really sorry. I messed up my life and probably yours and Annie's. Do you think you'll ever forgive me?"

"It's too late to ask for forgiveness."

J.T. began to cry again. Brett had an urge to console him or punch him, but he couldn't bring himself to do either. He just sat and let J.T. get hold of himself. J.T. got up, went into the bathroom, and came out with a box of Kleenex. "Sorry Brett, I'm not really asking for sympathy."

Brett waited again until J.T. was ready to continue. "I'm guessing that Claude flew you to someplace across the border and dropped you off. Where was it, Imperial?"

"Not exactly, we had to go through Mexican customs first, but a hundred bucks to the agent on the ramp and another hundred into the drawer got us through without any questions. You were right about stopping at Imperial. Claude has a hangar there where we unloaded his crates. After Imperial, Claude dropped me in Palm Springs and then he flew back to Calexico to check in with US customs. I caught a plane to Denver."

The front door opened and Maria came into the house. The expression of fear which had been on her face when she left was now replaced with one of anger. She headed for the bedroom and said to J.T., "Tony, can we talk?"

J.T. followed her into the bedroom and closed the

door. Brett couldn't hear all of the conversation; however, he picked up some of it. "What did you get me into? That guy knows everything, doesn't he? We're going to go to prison, I know it."

"We don't know that. I know him. He's got plenty of reasons to turn us in, but he's not the kind of guy who'll do it just for spite."

She was becoming hysterical. "Let's give the money back.'

"It's too late for that."

Maria was sobbing uncontrollably as J.T. came back into the living room. "Well Brett, what are you going to do? Are you going to call the FBI?"

J.T. was standing, so Brett got up off the couch to face him. "Is there any reason why I shouldn't?"

"There are lots of them and you know it. Can I ask that you sleep on it tonight and weigh the consequences of whatever action you decide on?"

"What if I decide to expose the whole thing?"

"Then I ask that you leave Maria out of it, and I'll go back to San Francisco with you."

Brett thought about it. He really wasn't sure what to do. Maybe a day to think it over would help him make the right decision. "Okay, do you want me to come by here in the morning?"

"I don't think this is the best atmosphere for that discussion. There's a Starbucks on the corner where you turned onto Edgewood. How about ten tomorrow morning?"

Brett started for the door. J.T. thrust out his hand, but Brett ignored it. "Ten o'clock at

Starbucks."

Brett drove back to the main boulevard he had taken off the interstate a couple hours earlier. He spotted a sign for Motel 6 and pulled into the lot. After paying the forty-two dollars in advance, he went to his room, threw his overnight case on the chair and flopped onto the bed.

J.T. was right. He had a lot to think about before making a decision. There were emotional, ethical, moral, and financial considerations which had already began to rip at his brain.

He no longer felt he owed anything to J.T., and he wouldn't lose any sleep over turning him in. Annie, however, was a different story. Turning J.T. over to the authorities would expose her to personal and public humiliation. He didn't know if he could do that. She was a much stronger woman than the one he had married, but would she be strong enough to stand up to this?

He had the urge to just give J.T. a pass, keep the secret to himself, and go on with his life, but both the ethical and moral issues tore at him. J.T. had committed insurance fraud along with several other crimes. Brett's silence would probably make him an accomplice.

Then there were the financial considerations. It was bad enough Annie would have to return the insurance proceeds, but she would still have to pay off J.T.'s credit card debts totaling nearly $200,000. All of the money Brett had paid her over the last five years would be gone. Brett, of course, would have to return the payout from the aircraft policy and accept the fact that he wouldn't be able to replace the Baron.

He tossed and turned all night; he couldn't make a decision. It really came down to whether he was going let Annie get blindsided by J.T.'s betrayal or whether he would keep a dark dirty secret for the rest of his life.

Brett hadn't had breakfast. He arrived at Starbucks a half hour early and ordered a tall coffee and a bagel with cream cheese. The most important decision of his life was going to be made at the last minute after talking to J.T. one more time.

As he finished up his bagel and was refilling his coffee, he glanced at his watch. It was ten fifteen, and J.T. hadn't yet arrived. By ten thirty Brett was pretty sure J.T. wasn't going to show, and at ten forty-five he went to the parking lot and started up his car.

Just as he had done yesterday, Brett knocked on the door of J.T.'s apartment. There was no response. He knocked again, but unlike the day before no one answered. A young woman in the apartment next door, who obviously had heard the knocking, came out into the hallway. "Can I help you?"

"I had an appointment with the Russos, but it doesn't look like anyone's around."

"Oh, they must have forgotten. They left last night. It looked like they were going on a long trip; they had four or five suitcases with them."

Brett got back in the car and sat for twenty minutes just staring into the distance and thinking. The apologies and tears were all an act. J.T. had no intention of ever seeing Brett again and was just stalling for time before he fled. He started to laugh and then he spoke out loud. "Keep looking over your shoulder J.T. Someday someone will be there. I guess I should thank you, at least I didn't have to make a decision this morning."

Chapter Thirty-four

Brett dropped the car off and checked in at the ticket counter. The next flight to San Francisco was leaving at two o'clock; it would get him back at three-thirty California time.

He had an hour and half to kill and went into the bookstore to pick up a copy of the San Francisco *Chronicle.* In section 'D', the Arts and Entertainment section, he spotted an ad for a concert at the HP Pavilion in San Jose. Brett rifled through his bag and located his cell phone. He dialed Annie's number. "Hi Annie, it's me."

"Brett, where are you?"

"I'm in Colorado waiting for a plane out of Denver.

"I couldn't sleep last night. I guess I was worried about you."

Brett smiled into the phone. "I'm fine; I'll be home by four o'clock. Hey, do you remember what I said to you when we first met at the fraternity?"

Annie smiled to herself in the mirror. "Sure, you said, hi, I'm Neil Diamond, welcome to my concert."

"Well, I want to deliver on that concert. Can I pick you up at six?"

"I'll have to check my social calendar; it's been so full lately. Yup, I have an opening. See you here at six."

Brett had to pay the scalper $400 a piece for the tickets, but they were worth it: Section AA, Row 3, Seats a,b. They were seated in the third row on the right side of the stage. Another thirty feet and they could reach out and touch Neil.

The room reeked with nostalgia. Brett looked out at the auditorium and couldn't see a face under forty. People were laughing and crying as the singer went through his list of old favorites.

By the last encore the entire audience was silent. Brett and Annie were standing, holding hands and glued to the lyrics of the last song. "….but I got an emptiness deep inside that I try but it won't let me go, and I'm not a man that likes to swear, but I've never cared for the sound of being alone."

The crowd began an exodus from the auditorium as Brett and Annie made their way toward the parking lot. They were both silent with the words from the last song, feelings of emptiness and sounds of loneliness, echoing through their heads.

Brett stopped walking and put his arms around her waist. "Annie, after we made love in Italy I whispered in your ear that I love so much, but you were asleep and didn't hear me."

Annie reached up and locked her arms around Brett's neck. "I did hear you but, I wasn't ready to respond. I'm ready now and I know I want us to be together." She took his hand and pulled him in the direction of their car. "Let's go home," she said.

They left the car in the driveway of the townhouse, and entered through the front door. Annie walked through the living room touching the familiar furniture. As she looked back at Brett, a tear rolled down her cheek.

Brett took her hand. "Welcome home," he said as he sat her down on the couch and inched up next to her. He took a deep breath, swallowed hard and said, "Annie, I have to apologize. I've been keeping a painful secret from you."

Annie's smile disappeared. "What secret?"

"I need to tell you about my trip to Colorado. We have some tough decisions to make together."

My Thanks

To the *Chico Tuesday Afternoon Book Club*
for their time and critical evaluation of the
manuscript.

> *April Boyle*
> *Helen Carbonaro*
> *Pam Dakof*
> *Candyce Griswold*
> *Yolanda Holt*
> *Bev Paull*
> *Lorraine Rupp*

To *Carla Resnick* for her wonderful cover and
book design.

Special thanks to *Candyce Griswold* and
Bev Paull for their hours of relentless editing.

Author's Note

I felt a need to create the character of Brett Raven, when I realized the profession of dentistry was in desperate need of a fictional hero.

Dentists have been represented many times in books and movies, but always as either villains or buffoons. In *Marathon Man* and *Little Shop of Horrors* the dentist was a sadist who enjoyed inflicting pain. In *Mash*, the dentist was a boob they called Jawbreaker, and in *Hangover*, he was so stupid he pulled out his own front tooth.

I decided the protagonist in a mystery novel does not need to be a lawyer, ex-cop or medical examiner. As long as he is smart, resourceful, and courageous, he can emerge from any field or any profession. I hope Brett, a dentist, exhibited these traits and as a fictional hero neutralized some of the stereotypes attributed to his profession.

The dental and flying scenarios represented actual procedures used in both fields, but all of the characters in the book, including Brett, are fictional and any resemblance to real people is coincidental.

FOLLOW MIKE PAULL ON:

Facebook

Linkedin

Skyhawk Publishing.com

E-book format available from:

Amazon.com

Barnes & Noble.com

AppleStore.com

www.ingramcontent.com/pod-product-compliance
Lightning Source LLC
Chambersburg PA
CBHW020602110726
47899CB00002B/333